LUCKY STRIKE

CATE BEAUMONT

Hey, Vicky!
I hope you
get Lucky!
Cate Beaumont

Sirena Press, LLC

Published in the United States of America by

Sirena Press LLC ©2017

Cover Art by Scott Carpenter

Lucky Strike: Book 1 in the Lucky, Kentucky Series

Ebook ISBN: 978-1-947145-00-9

Print ISBN: 978-1-947145-01-6

Lucky Strike, Book 1 in the Lucky, Kentucky Saga

She Wants a Fling...

Kelsey Taggert is a modern woman blazing her way through single parenthood. While running her own business, she has no time for love since her cheating ex-husband left her for a stripper. A brush with death motivates her to step out of her comfort zone and get started on a Bucket List of new experiences. Number one on her list...a hot love affair.

He Wants The Real Thing...

Workaholic Deke Connelly saves Kelsey's life when she is struck by lightning, but she is not the only one electrified by the experience. He can't stop thinking about the feisty brunette that dropped unexpectedly into his life. He believes she could be the one. Now how to convince her?

Can the spark of their new relationship survive the shadows of their past?

CHAPTER ONE

Kelsey Taggert stumbled out of the eye doctor's tinted glass door and into the gloomy afternoon's light drizzling rain. Even the meager gray glow that filtered through the heavily overcast sky pierced her poor dilated pupils like the glow of a thousand suns. She winced at the glare penetrating her sunglasses, lifted her hand to shade her eyes, and searched the strip mall parking lot for her car.

Her cell phone chimed her mother's ringtone just as she was placing her order for updated lenses and new contacts. Her son Charlie was sitting on her parents' front porch, sobbing his six-year-old heart out, and refusing to come in out of the rain. He kept insisting that his daddy was "just late" and even the promise of ice cream hadn't lured him inside, so her parents were calling to see what they should do.

Once again, her good for nothing, mangy canine of an ex-husband had conveniently "forgotten" to pick up their son for his Saturday visitation—the first Saturday he had managed to schedule in the last three weeks.

This morning, as Kelsey left her son with her parents to head out for a long-overdue optometrist appointment, she had texted the THIRD reminder to Brad about where to pick their son up. Since he worked for a used car lot a few blocks from her childhood home, it should have been convenient. It also should have happened two hours ago.

Brad was notoriously late for everything. Kelsey's parents didn't panic for the first half hour. Just as Kelsey was being ushered into an exam room and recovering from the vicious "puff" of air that some businesslike vision tech had just blasted into her unsuspecting eyeball, Kelsey got the first uneasy text from her mom, letting her know that Brad was, once again, late. As another half hour passed with Kelsey sitting in a cushy exam recliner and struggling to read a slightly blurry book on her Kindle phone app without her contacts in, she got another text notification ding from her mother to let her know that Charlie was getting antsy and that Brad was a no-show. About five minutes after Dr. Kenner's nurse had dripped the chilly dilation drops into Kelsey's neglected eyes, Kelsey got another, more urgent message, letting her know that Brad wasn't picking up his phone and that Charlie was getting really upset. Kelsey shot off a response at the end of her blessedly short conference with Dr. Kenner, promising to be there as soon as she could. She called her ex-husband several different species of ugly animal mutations as she forced her own sunglasses over the plastic sun shields offered by the front desk receptionist and rushed for the exit, making a mental note to call and order her contacts later. The jackass-alope only had every other weekend visitation rights. It was absolutely ridiculous that he couldn't manage to remember he was a father two days out of the month.

Kelsey started dialing Brad's cell number as she exited the office reception area, but the call went directly to his voicemail. She jogged carefully across the puddle strewn asphalt parking lot as fast as her wedge heeled espadrilles would carry her toward her car. She forced her poor eyes to focus on her cell phone, scrolling through her contacts and glancing at the ground. She *knew* she shouldn't have worn her new summer sandals out when the sky was threatening rain from all of those huge grey clouds. Just as she found the listing to call the dealership where Brad sold used cars, her foot sank into a warm wet puddle full of murky rain water. She groaned as she pulled her foot out of the puddle and watched the dirty brown water drip off of the once pristine white linen. Great... just perfect. She shook the water off as best she could and walked the remaining three feet to the car as she pushed the buttons necessary to connect her call.

"Ed Stern Automotive. How may I direct your call?"

"Alice? This is Kelsey Taggert. Could I speak with Brad, please?"

"Hi, Kelsey," Alice answered warmly. "I'm sorry, but Brad isn't here. He left about an hour ago for the home-blessing and walk-through at his new house." As Alice described the Pagan sage burning ritual that Brad's new girl friend "just insisted would make the house a happy one," Kelsey's blood pressure started to rise. "Do you want to leave a message?"

Kelsey let out a frustrated breath. Of COURSE he had blown their son off for his bimbo. Her blood began to boil, but she knew she had to remain calm to get anything out of Alice. Since the divorce, Kelsey had successfully maintained her dignity when interacting with the people in Brad's circle. She believed that you caught more flies with honey than vinegar, but some folks were clearly on the Brad side of the fence. Alice was sweet and had always liked Kelsey. The older woman was well-aware that Brad left her for his current female companion, so she was bound to be a little sympathetic to Kelsey's situation.

"No, but thanks, Alice," she chirped in her most upbeat, happy-go-lucky, divorcee not about to kill her ex-husband voice. Her voice was so forcibly sweet that she was giving herself a cavity. No way could Alice tell that she was about to commit a felony against a certain former husband.

Think, Kelsey...THINK, she silently screamed at herself. An idea popped into her head. "I was supposed to meet him to pick up Charlie, but I had an appointment run over. He must have taken Charlie with him to the ceremony. Can you give me the address of the new house? I'll just meet him there."

"Sure. It's 144 Spiral Drive, " Alice promptly rattled off. She even mentioned a few helpful cross-streets to get Kelsey there without a hitch. Kelsey thanked Alice and slowly pulled her old gold Honda Accord out into the busy suburban traffic. Just as she turned onto the main thoroughfare through town, huge rain drops began splattering her dusty windshield. The rain just about made it possible for her to drive with her pupils as big as man-hole covers.

She barely managed to drive the three miles from the doctor's office to the rotten bastard's brand new house construction site at the posted thirty-five miles per hour speed limit, but the last thing she needed was to have her full head of Pissed Off Momma steam wasted on some poor, unsuspecting police officer trying to ticket her for speeding. Chances where low that any cop was going to brave the steadily increasing storm to give her a ticket for ten-over the posted speed limit, but it wasn't worth the risk. She would definitely see the inside of a jail cell if she had to deal with a traffic stop right now.

Kelsey turned off the main street onto a brand new thoroughfare marked by a huge stone arch. “The Retreat” was carved into the arch's capstone. How pretentious! The high-end construction site was located next to a turkey farm and a water sanitation plant.

In the late 1700's, their little town of Lucky, Kentucky,

located directly across the historic Ohio river from Cincinnati, Ohio, had been settled as a trading center for the wine, pork and tobacco industries that flourished along the fertile river valley. Its position on the waterfront left very little land for new housing construction. Folks tended to build wherever they could find available land. This particular subdivision was a former pig farm. While the previous residents had smelled almost as bad as their feathered neighbors, the new home owners would never be able to open their windows to catch a cool breeze from the nearby river. Good luck "retreating" from the smell of a thousand free-range turkeys.

Maybe the subdivision's name served as a counterpoint of the water treatment plant...'treat' and 'retreat?' Nonetheless, all the houses in the exclusive enclave were three-story showplaces with tiny manicured lawns meant to impress visitors without requiring homeowners to perform menial tasks like mowing grass, cleaning gutters or speaking to neighbors. Where Kelsey's cozy little two-bedroom Cape Cod boasted a coveted carport, these stucco showplaces sported three car garages and home security system placards.

Kelsey parked in front of the construction lot with the number matching the address Alice had rattled off and looked up and down the street for Brad's "new to him" Mercedes. When she didn't see it, she left the car, ducking to avoid the huge rain drops pummeling the ground. Clutching her cell phone in one hand and repeatedly hitting redial on her jack-monkey ex-husband's cell phone number, Kelsey sprinted up the unpaved drive toward the front door. The uneven driveway, slick with rain, slowed her mad dash to the shelter of the framed-in front porch, soaking her to the skin. As she tried to dial Brad's cell phone one last time, the phone clicked to his now-familiar voicemail message just as a blinding flash and a searing jolt of pain engulfed her body like fire. The burning sensation lasted only a few seconds before blessed darkness overcame her.

Kelsey slowly opened her eyes and saw nothing but.... clouds. The dark gray masses covering the Kentucky sky filtered most of the sun's light to a dull yellowish glow. Kelsey tried to blink raindrops from her vision and rolled her aching head to the side. Why was she lying on the ground? The overcast sun wasn't producing much light, but even that weak glare increased the throbbing drumbeat behind her eyes. She squeezed her eyes shut and tried to narrow down what part of her aching body hurt the most. God, what was that *pounding* on her head? Oh, wait...maybe that *was* her head. Jeez Louise, she must be *really* hung over if her head was already pounding. What in the name of all that was holy had her friends let her do?

Kelsey groaned and tried to shift to a more comfortable position, but the ground was not getting any softer. She felt like her body had been smashed beneath a steam roller and there was something warm running down her thumping forehead. She tried to lift her hand to wipe rainwater from her face, but her arm seemed stuck in something on the ground. She groaned and yanked with what energy she could muster and her arm flew into the air with a sucking sound. Oh. My. GOD! Was that MUD? She mentally vowed on a stack of Mr. T's Bartender Bibles to *kill* whichever of her so-called friends had let her drink this much...*Tequila?* That's the only explanation, but where was everyone else? They wouldn't have left her somewhere...alone...her friends would never do that. Kelsey's hand hovered just short of wiping her eyes when a gooey cold blob of mud landed on her face. More mud fell across her face and Kelsey stopped short of actually touching her aching head.

Somewhere beyond her feet, Kelsey heard, "Honey! Honey, are you okay?" Who was calling for his "honey"? The muddy ground vibrated with the approach of running footfalls. Who was he talking to?

Kelsey closed her eyes against the falling rain and tried to get her bearings. The vibration of someone's approaching feet cease right next to her head and someone brushed her cheek with a calloused hand.

"Sugar, can you hear me? Can you open your eyes?" The gruff voice wasn't familiar, but it was definitely masculine and it seemed truly concerned. Maybe Honey and Sugar were his dogs. The only thing those ridiculous names could possibly belong to would be those obnoxious little yappy dogs that women carried around in purses and kissed on the lips...yuck!

Kelsey managed to get her left eye open to a mere slit and squinted at the figure blocking the incessant rain. As she began to focus, a ruggedly handsome face began to take shape. The man's hair was dark as night with skin tanned from the outdoors. She opened both eyes wide, but was instantly stabbed with pain from the light and slammed them closed again. She cracked her eyes open slightly and stared...hard. Recognition niggled at the front of her mind, but she was having trouble focusing. Suddenly it hit her..... "Loki?" she asked, incredulously.

Her black haired giant didn't answer, only ran his fingers gently over her scalp making her feel deliciously drowsy. His fingers skimmed her neck and shoulder. If only he would move that massage a little lower, he might actually rid her neck of the kink that came from crouching over a laptop all day long. When the giant man-god's hands hit the egg shaped lump on the side of her head, Kelsey let out an involuntary groan of pain. Everything hurt and she didn't want to move, even if a hunky man-god did the moving for her.

"Sorry, Honey. I just needed to see where you were hurt." Kelsey tried scrunching her nose in distaste at the silly nick-name, but even the small effort it would take to move those little facial muscles seemed beyond her abilities at that moment. She just wanted to sleep. Even a short nap in a cold puddle seemed like heaven right then. Heaven? Was she in Heaven?

"Is this Valhalla? Am I dead? Are they lime?" she heard a whispery voice ask. It took her a second to realize that she had spoken her musings out loud to the God of Mischief. He looked at her with confusion and frowned. Oh, no, Kelsey thought, I have angered the god. Maybe he didn't like limes?

"Or maybe like green grapes....that would look more like eyeballs...but limes go with tequila...Hey! Where's your hammer?" Kelsey's voice faded and her eyes became too heavy to keep open. She closed her lids and pictured the delicious dark-haired Son of Odin feeding her Key Lime Pie and shots of tequila on a picnic blanket in the Elysian Fields...but wait... wasn't that Greek heaven? Would Loki be in Greek heaven? He didn't have a hammer...Thor did! That must be why he was frowning. That made sense! Oh, her head ached too much to think about it now. Maybe a nap now and flirting with the man-god later.

"Honey, don't go to sleep! Stay awake! The ambulance is coming!" Kelsey felt someone lift her head and shoulders, presumably, the pretty bright-eyed Norseman, but all she could really think about was how she had gotten into a mud pit and why she felt so weak and horrible. The water from the mud and the incessant rain had saturated her jeans and cash-mere sweater and she started to tremble uncontrollably. Loki wrapped something warm around her. The makeshift blanket smelled like citrus and new lumber from the hardware store.

"You even smell like limes!" Kelsey babbled. "Did we do some body shots? You are a Pretty Man!....pretty, pretty Pie Man...." Her thoughts of pie reminded her of her ex-husband.

"Did you hit me in the head with your brother's Big Hammer?" A giggle bubbled up. "I said 'Big Hammer,' but you might only have a small hammer. Too bad you didn't hit Brad with your little hammer instead of my head." She was pretty sure that she was HILARIOUS right now. The Pretty Man didn't laugh, though. "I hate Key Lime Pie because of Barbie's boobs. No more tequila, either. Sorry." He did not think she was funny?

He just kept her head propped against his lap and sheltered her from the pelting rain. He held her hand in one of his big calloused ones and, with the other, rubbed her shoulders in soothing circles, but said nothing. Typical god....never an answer for mere humans, Kelsey thought. She heard the distinct sound of sirens wailing in the distance, the sound coming closer and closer.

Soon, the sirens blared nearby and lights flashed behind her closed eyelids. As the roar of the siren went silent, a door slammed and squishing noises grew louder as footsteps moved closer to where she was trying to lie as still as possible to dull the thunking in her head. Kelsey noticed a muffled static of walkie-talkies proceed a new voice that spoke above her.

"What do we have here?" The new voice was male and gruff.

"Looked like she was struck by lightning," said Kelsey's Nordic God Umbrella. "Damnedest thing I've ever seen!"

"Were you injured, Sir?" enquired the gruff voice.

"No, I'm fine. I wasn't near her when it happened. I'm the General Contractor on this job site. I was sitting in my truck across the street when I saw her head toward the house here talking on the phone. I saw a bright flash and heard a loud

BOOM! Next thing I know, she's lying on the ground here, not moving. I called 911 as I was running over, but my phone battery died during the call. I wasn't sure you guys got the location. I haven't moved her except to lift her head and shoulders out of the mud." As Kelsey's head thumped, her rescuer talked on and on.

"Ma'am, can you hear me?" asked the gruffest of the voices as he lifted Kelsey's eyelids with gloved fingertips and shined what felt like a laser into her brain. She groaned at the increased discomfort and attempted to squeeze her eyes tightly shut to block the nasty man's death ray. A new set of hands moved over her and she winced when the not-so-gentle gloved animal paws hit the lump on the side of her throbbing head.

"She opened her eyes for a few seconds, but couldn't keep them open," Kelsey's Man-God explained. "She mumbled something about tequila and limes, but she doesn't smell like she's been drinking. I tried to keep her awake, but she hasn't really moved since I got here." Kelsey's dreamy green-eyed savior wrapped up his story without letting her head slip from his lap.

As the Fire and Rescue paramedics surrounded her and continued their initial check for injuries, her citrus-scented savior continued to support her neck and head with his big, warm hands. The only part of her body that felt warm was the area in contact with the brunette stranger's comforting touch. She frowned when he had to let her go. As the paramedics began to lift her gurney into the ambulance for her trip to the E.R., Kelsey's lingering regret was that she had to give up temptations now, since Loki looked so tasty....

CHAPTER TWO

Kelsey slowly woke to the incessant buzz of whispering and a thump of pain that moved through her body with each beat of her heart. She was lying down with her eyes tightly closed, the unsavory scents of antiseptic and heavily starched laundry that reminded her of the nursing home she used to visit during her High School service project. Where was she? She recognized the hushed voices of women animatedly trying to speak softly and hovering around her bed. Sunlight streamed in through a nearby window, bright enough to make her think it was late morning or early afternoon. At least the rain had stopped. She remembered waking up to rain on her face the last time she opened her eyes. What was going on? She tried to lift an arm to rub her thumping temples, but she couldn't seem to get her aching muscles to cooperate, and barely succeeded in moving her hand from her stomach to her side.

Even though sounds were becoming more distinct—some machine wouldn't stop beeping--Kelsey was afraid to open her eyes. All the foot shuffling, pacing and whispering reminded her of a funeral. One cadence reminded her of

Lyssie. And the one who answered was definitely Cat. Two of her best friends were here, but it felt more like the "morning after" than a party. Kelsey loved cocktails with the ladies, but couldn't remember going out last night, much less how she had gotten here...wherever "here" was. A set of clicking heels stopped by the head of her stiff, uncomfortable bed.

"Be quiet, now. You are going to wake her!" hissed Della Sandfoss, her first best friend from Kindergarten. "Fucking loudmouth!" Della, an accountant, had owned a small firm with her husband Dave until his untimely death in a car accident last year. Dave left her with a business, no life insurance and two busy little boys who broke anything they touched. Strangers mistook her for a librarian in her conservative suits and low-heeled shoes, but her favorite word was "fuck" and she worked it into every conversation at least once, more frequently when she was upset. Clearly, she was upset about something.

"Jesus Christ on a saltine cracker, Della, YOU be quiet! You're the one hissing in her ear," was the stage whispered response from Cat. Catherine Marston, an attorney, took no shit from *anyone*. She tore holes in pompous lawyers for a living and did not know the meaning of "inside voice." She also constantly harassed Della for being the most senior member of their group at the ripe old age of forty-one. Cat only lagged behind Della by four months, but she was holding onto forty like a winning lottery ticket. Catherine Marston did NOT have a squishy center, but she had a soft spot for underdogs and would go to the mat for any woman in the hospital room with her.

"Ladies! Enough! She's waking up." Lysandra Prescott picked up Kelsey's hand and began patting it softly. "Kelsey? Do you know who I am?" she asked. The other three women crowded around the bed and touched some part of Kelsey's her blanket-covered body.

"Of course I know who you are! Why would you ask me that?" Kelsey's scratchy throat only produced a whisper, but it was enough to release four deeply held sighs from the surrounding women. "Are you thirsty, Kelsey? Can I get you a drink of water? Are you in pain? Do you want some pain medication?"

Kelsey slowly opened her eyes, blinked against the painful sunlight and instinctively turned her head away. Lyssie dropped her hand and held three fingers up in front of Kelsey's face.

"How many fingers am I holding up? Do you know where you are?" Lyssie's thin, high-pitched demands contrasted her normal smooth, calm tone.

"Are you kidding me, Lys?" snapped Janie. "The doctors said she had a shock and a head injury. Give her a second to wake up."

"Sorry, Kels! I have just been so worried." Lyssie frantically fanned her hands in front of her eyes, as though she were drying tears before they could roll down her cheeks. Lysandra Prescott was a crier-- an ugly, snot-slinging bawler who was impossible to reign-in until she had dehydrated. Luckily for the rest of the group, Janie carried tissues.

Jayne Smith, their most practical friend, even sported a practical name. She was the youngest of the group at thirty-seven, but she carried an old soul. She had a purse that, in any emergency, could supply a Doomsday prepper for a week in complete comfort. Janie sat down and plopped her enormous carry-all onto her lap. After rooting around in her Tardis purse for a few seconds, Janie handed Lyssie a couple tissues and then stood and began straightening the covers on Kelsey's hospital bed.

"The doctor said you will probably have a headache for a few days, but that your heart rhythm seems consistent and you don't have any bad burns," Janie stated in a matter-of-fact tone.

Kelsey's eyes grew wider with every word Janie said Then she went light-headed and wasn't sure if she'd heard right.

"Heart rhythm? BURNS? What the hell does my heart have to do with my headache?" Kelsey asked the room at large. "All I remember is waking up on the ground...in the mud. I must have fallen. Why would I have burns from falling down?"

All four of her friends looked at each other, then almost simultaneously turned to look at her with the most serious expressions she had seen since the last time someone's husband had died. Kelsey's heart sank. This was B.A.D.

"Kels, you were struck by lightning yesterday. You were at the building site for Brad and Barbie's new house."

Kelsey stared at Della. She knew her friend was speaking English, but the words did not compute. Cat piped up next.

"Apparently, you were standing in the front yard talking on your cell phone when the lightning hit you. Some guy from the builder's crew saw it happen and called for an ambulance. He saved your life!"

Her friends watched silently as Kelsey tried to process the information. "What in the hell was I doing there? Why would I be at Brad and the Bimbo's new love shack?"

"We don't know," said Lyssie, "but the hospital called your mom, since she was listed as your emergency contact person on the card in your wallet. She called Della, who called the rest of us, and here we are. The doctor just stopped in and checked on you. He said you were doing fine, so we sent your mom home. She has been here all night with you, but since you're okay, she wanted to get home to your dad and Charlie."

"Is Charlie okay? Did my mom tell him what happened?" Kelsey asked anxiously. Oh my god! He would be so scared.

Charlie was too little to understand what had happened to her.

"Your mom told him that you had been struck by lightning, but that you were fine and that the doctors wanted to watch you for a little while to see what happened next," Jayne explained. "He seemed to think it was pretty cool and started cheering that you were going to be a superhero now, so prepare yourself." Kelsey and the other girls chuckled quietly. "Cat was sure you had seen Elvis and only came back to confirm his actual death to the world." She laughed.

"I never said that," Cat said. "I said *maybe* she would be able to answer some of the great questions that plague mankind! I said *nothing* about The King in particular!" Kelsey relaxed back against her flat hospital pillow as the good-natured debate raged on around her. The familiar cadence of her friends' voices calmed her initial panic and her muscles began to relax after the shock of finding out about her accident.

Just as Kelsey started to ask if anyone knew about the guy that helped her at the building site, a knock on her partially opened door halted her question. Conversation stopped as five pairs of eyes turned toward a large man dressed in a green-and-blue plaid shirt and worn jeans who hesitated in the doorway. Her gaze locked with a pair of eerily familiar, bright green eyes. Kelsey's cheeks warmed with embarrassment. She would recognize those eyes anywhere. Apparently, she had not been dreaming when she met the God of Mischief in a rainstorm. She knew she was gawking, but couldn't look away. She certainly recognized his face, but struggled to recall his name.

All of the women continued to stare without saying a word, but Kelsey couldn't blame them for their rudeness. She couldn't take her eyes off him, either. The man was beautiful. His six-foot, four-inch frame filed the doorway. With wavy black hair and skin tanned from long hours in the sun, he looked like a bronzed god. His linebacker shoulders eclipsed the overhead light as he began walking toward her on two muscle-bound thighs hugged by worn denim. His work boots made soft thunks as they carried him toward Kelsey's bed.

"Hi there. Are you Kelsey?" The stranger asked tentatively.

All Kelsey could do was nod, but immediately regretted that maneuver when the previously thumping ache across her forehead became a stabbing pain. She squeezed her eyes closed and held her body still, willing the pain to recede. Della was the only one who could seem to muster a voice in the presence of such delicious manliness.

"Yes, she's Kelsey. Who are you?" Della asked in a slightly breathless voice.

As the stabbing receded to a dull ache, Kelsey tentatively opened her eyes to see the man staring intently at her.

"I'm Deacon Connelly. After I saw you light up my work-site yesterday, I wanted to stop by and see for myself that you were okay." He held his hand toward Kelsey. "You can call me Deke." When he saw her wince as she tried to lift her hand to his, he reached down and took her hand like he had been holding it for years.

"Hi, Deke. Have we met before....I mean, before yesterday? You look so familiar..." Kelsey said.

Deke's strong, calloused hand gave hers a gentle squeeze before he released her. Her fingers felt chilled after the warmth of his touch, and she felt a little bereft, which was a totally weird reaction to a complete stranger!

"Not formally, but I figured we should be introduced since you took a couple of years off my life and all!" Deke laughed quietly and his eyes crinkled in good humor. "I asked the guys down at the firehouse who were on your ambulance run if they knew who you were so I could check up on you."

Della broke in indignantly, “They just released confidential patient information to you because you asked? They should never have done that!” The ladies all sucked in horrified breaths at their friend’s outburst, but Deke gave a small laugh and shook his head.

“No, ma’am, not confidential from me. I’m the general contractor on the worksite where the accident happened. I’m responsible for any accidents on my watch."

“Ha!” Della responded. “You are just here to cover your ass! Kelsey, don’t say ANYTHING to him! He works for Brad the Bastard and Boobs! He is just here to keep you from suing his lying, cheating, broke ass!”

Kelsey winced at the loud outburst and Della icy glare softened as she turned toward the hospital bed. "Sorry, Kels! I get carried away."

Deke raised his hands, palms outward, his face flushed. "No, Ma'am. That's not it at all. I was the one that saw the accident and I just wanted to make sure she was all right."

Jayne and Lyssie glanced at each other and raised their eyebrows as if to say, "Maybe this hot man is actually interested in our friend." Big, strong construction men didn’t blush for nothing.

Cat noticed the eyebrow sign language and watched Kelsey stare at the man with the telltale flush. Kelsey was gripping the sheets and had a little furrow between her eyebrows as she stared intently at Deke's face. When he wasn't looking, Cat caught Kelsey running her eyes all over Deke's hot body, but she made sure to avert her hot gaze as soon as he moved his head in her direction. She tried to get Della's attention by bumping her foot, but Della continued to glare at Deke. It had been so long since Kelsey had shown any level of interest in a man that Cat knew she and the girls were going to have to give her a chance.

“Sorry, Kels,” Della whispered with an apologetic grimace.

"Della, Can't you see the guy is concerned?" Cat snapped.. "C'mon, ladies. Let's go get coffee and something decent for Kelsey to eat while she talks to the tasty hero dude."

Kelsey sent her friend a horrified glance. How freaking embarrassing! Cat just called the man "tasty"...right in front of him! She glanced back at Deke to see how offended he was, but he wore a good-natured smirk. She didn't bother to apologize for them. They were tactless hussies, but they were *her* tactless hussies, and she didn't really care what other people thought...mostly... Deke seemed to understand that any apology would ring hollow anyway. Those ladies had spunk.

The girls gathered their purses and gave Kelsey waves and promises of returning with something edible as they filed out of the room. Cat, as the last one out, pulled the door closed behind her with a wink and a flirty finger wave. Even before the door closed, they were bickering about where they would have lunch. Kelsey watched them leave and then returned her attention to the man beside her bed.

Deke stood beside the bed rail and stared intently at her. He seemed to take stock of her as she lay clutching the thin hospital blanket to her chest in a vain attempt to cover her hideous hospital gown. Since the last thing she remembered before waking up in the hospital was lying in a mud puddle, she doubted that he was too impressed with what he saw . She wore one of those horrible dull blue paisley hospital gowns and cringed at the thought of what her little run-in with Mother Nature had done to her makeup. Her shoulder-length wavy chocolate hair probably hid the two little dimples that appeared when she smiled or grimaced. Too bad her present grimace resulted from pain. People said her dimples were "cute," and she would give just about *anything* for this man to think she was cute right now.

Her voice was scratchy but her tone was determined. "So you work at the building site where I was, uh, hurt?" Kelsey couldn't even *say* "struck by lightning" yet. It was too terrifying. "Did you see what happened? I don't remember much of anything except feeling cold and my head really hurting." Kelsey rushed on, trying to hide her embarrassment, "I didn't understand much, but I knew I wasn't alone. Thank you."

❦

Deke Connelly stood next to Kelsey's bed and kept his gaze steadily on her as she lay there, clutching the dingy white sheet and staring at him through narrowed, crystalline blue eyes ...the same remarkable blue that he'd glimpsed in the face of the muddy, unresponsive woman laying in the unfinished front yard of his building site.

"Yes," Deke confirmed, "I am the general contractor at the site. I was just wrapping up my final inspection when I saw your car pull up to the lot across from my truck. You scared the crap out of me when I saw that flash and then you lying on the ground."

Deke glanced around the room and then grabbed the only chair and pulled it closer to the bed. He sat down and leaned his elbows on his knees, feigning a relaxed, non-threatening pose, when all he wanted was to grab her hand. The way she repeatedly clenched and unclenched her hands in the blankets made him think she was skittish, and he thought sitting down might make her more comfortable. Lord knows, he was used to people being intimidated by his size. Sometimes that was an advantage he used to keep people honest, but he didn't' want to discomfort the petite woman in front of him. All he wanted was to comfort her. He couldn't remember ever wanting to soothe a woman before, but then again, he had never seen someone almost die in front of him.

"You were pretty out of it. You kept saying something

about fruit and tequila and, pardon my language, but someone's boobs. Does any of this ring a bell?"

A blush rose from the neck of Kelsey's drab blue hospital gown to her forehead. "I actually said that ... out loud? Oh, God! I'm so embarrassed." Kelsey fluttered her hand, as if to swat the embarrassing words away, but immediately grimaced and clutched her head. "I remember thinking that your eyes were such a bright green that they reminded me of Key Lime Pie..." Kelsey's voice faded, as if she didn't know how to continue without further embarrassing herself. She wouldn't look at him, but Deke kept staring, willing her to meet his gaze.

"Pie, huh? Well, that explains why you were calling me Pie Eyes. Did you really mean it when you said you hated pie?" Kelsey turned pinker and Deke started to chuckle. That blush of hers made him start to think of other ways he could get her color up. Even though her dark brown hair was tangled and her eye makeup was smudged under her eyes, there was something about this woman that turned Deke's crank. She was sexy as hell, but not her appearance alone. She was a natural beauty, and her lack of artifice meant she had no idea how attractive she was. She wasn't the empty-headed, flirty type who threw themselves in his lap whether he was out looking or not. They usually wanted him for his body or his wallet. When they discovered he was willing to burn up the sheets but unwilling to shop for rings, those ladies moved on without looking back. As simple as those hook-ups were, they left him wanting more...and Kelsey appeared to have "more" in spades.

Kelsey covered her blushing cheeks and mumbled through her fingers, "I am so embarrassed. I like pie just fine. I mean, I like Key Lime Pie, but I don't usually tell people what kind of food they remind me of! Oh my god, I am so embarrassed."

Deke laughed quietly and reached over the bed rails to take her small, soft hand into his. When she didn't pull away, he hoped that meant she was relaxing in his presence.

"Well, despite the fact that you shortened my life by about one year for every second it took me to reach you and make sure you were alive, it was certainly worth it to see those dimples."

Kelsey narrowed her eyes at him in confusion, trying to figure out his angle.

"My dimples, huh?" she asked.

"Yep. They were pretty cute when you were going on and on about how much you wanted to eat pie with me." He grinned at her confusion, wanting to make her blush. "What do you say we go get some pie when they spring you from this joint?"

Kelsey's hand stiffened in his grasp and she pulled away, sighing as she met Deke's gaze. " After the whole Loki/pie thing, I guess you imagine I'm brain damaged, but I assure you I'm fine. Thank you for checking on me." A shield dropped over her formerly expressive face. "I am sorry I interrupted your day. You can get back to whatever you should be doing. I have health insurance, so I won't be suing you or anything."

Deke's back stiffened. "I'm not here because I was worried about a lawsuit. I wanted to make sure you were okay. Also, I found the phone you were talking on when the lightning stuck. It came through the storm a bit worse for wear." Deke removed a muddy hunk of black and silver plastic wrapped in a zippered sandwich bag from his pocket.

She tentatively reached for the baggie of cracked glass and plastic. Her face went ashen and her eyes seemed to glaze as she clutched the small bag to her chest. Deke gave silent thanks that only her phone was mangled. She shuddered and blinked to try to dry the tears pooling in her eyes, but a pair of salty droplets escaped and ran down her pale cheeks. Deke's voice seemed to bring her back to the here and now.

"You're okay, Kelsey," he said, and her eyes refocused. "You're all right, Kelsey." Deke's voice softened, "Do you work for the city or county? I wasn't aware of any additional, scheduled inspections. The paramedics said your last name was Taggert. Are you related to Brad?"

She shuddered and looked up. "Not anymore, thank God! He's my ex, which is why I went there in the first place. His girlfriend is the one building that house. He was supposed to pick up our son yesterday, but never showed, and I was trying to catch him and give him a piece of my mind before he disappeared for the day."

Kelsey's voice got angrier with each word. "When he left our son crying on my parents' porch, his secretary told me he wasn't there because he and his new girlfriend had scheduled a home blessing and cleansing at their new place during the whatever-Crazy-Bitch-phase the moon was in. It is one thing to forget you made plans, but to blow a six-year-old off to placate your nasty skank sugar mama is just too much! I snapped. I drove over to the house site to have it out with him. I mean, he hasn't made a child support payment in three months, and now he doesn't bother to come get Charlie after making plans with him! He is only six years old! He doesn't understand." Kelsey swiped at the angry tears rolling from her eyes. "I don't care if he falls off the face of the earth, but I will not stand for him being a deadbeat! If he can afford to build a new house with his new girlfriend, he can afford to contribute to our son's upbringing!" Kelsey must have realized she was yelling because she covered her mouth with her hand and winced. Deke processed this new information and realized that his next statement was going to hurt her as much as her outburst had.

❦

Other than a lift of his eyebrows, Kelsey's outburst didn't seem to faze Deke. He sat forward in the chair, staring intently into her eyes. Although he appeared a bit confused by her rant, Deke seemed *interested* in what she said, which was more than most men did when she dropped the ex-husband bomb.

Deke hesitated a moment, took a deep breath, and his previously light expression hardened with resolve. He opened his mouth, then closed it, then opened it again."You know he paid cash for the build, right?"

Kelsey froze. Had she heard him correctly? She stared, her mouth hanging open, but Deke's expression remained sober. She snapped her jaw shut. "He *what?*" she demanded in a deceptively quiet voice. Deke grimaced, but didn't look away. "Did you just say that he paid for the house upfront....*with cash?*"

"Well," Deke said, "*someone* paid cash for the build, and his name is on the paperwork as the owner. It's fairly unusual for someone to have enough cash in escrow to cover the entire cost of a luxury home, so it made quite an impression on my team. We aren't required to ask questions about where the money came from, but we figured it was an inheritance or something. I guess you don't know where the money came from either?"

Her mouth no longer hung open, but if she clenched her teeth any harder, she was going to crack a molar. She began taking deep breaths to find some elusive calm. In through her nose, out through her mouth, over and over, just like that little hippie crackpot had tried to teach her during her natural childbirth class. It didn't help any more now than it had when she'd shoved a ten pound, eight ounce future linebacker out of her body. Those natural childbirth assholes deserved a punch in the face, but not as big a punch as her ex deserved! She was mad enough to deliver a Tyson-esque knockout punch right now.

"The reserve for the build is almost used up, and they have made so many special modifications to the original plans that there is going to have to be another infusion of cash for us to proceed with the finish work. We had to stop everything and send the subs home yesterday after the fiancée said the bathrooms weren't *oriented* correctly." Deke rolled his eyes. "I stayed there to make sure the site was secure after the disagreement. I was just finishing up when you arrived."

Kelsey listened to every word and tried to get her tired, recently electrified brain to process the information bombs he dropped. If what he said was true, the Brastard had been holding out on her *and their son* for MONTHS! The longer she listened, the hotter her temper burned and the faster the monitor tracking her heart rate jumped. Kelsey inhaled sharply through her nose and slapped the bed with both open palms. Wait a second...did he just say..."Fiancée? They're freaking ENGAGED? I am going to punch that lying slime bag RIGHT in the NUTS the next time I see him! There won't be anything left of his man parts for Barbie to Feng-shui!" Kelsey's heart monitor was beeping frantically and she was breathing much too rapidly to keep the nurse's out of her room.

Deke raised both hands, palms out. "Now, hold up! There is no need to harm any man parts yet. I could be wrong about some of the details. Ms. Delacroix said something about moving in before the wedding. She's wearing a ring. I assumed she meant her own wedding. The file is back at my office and I haven't looked at the financial paperwork. My partner handles that part of the business. I mostly work off a work order and the project plan, which tracks spending. That is the only reason I know we've almost reached the original estimate, but funding information isn't listed there. Let me look into it further before you get any more riled up. You are supposed to be resting, and I just sent your heart rate to the moon. The nurse will be here any—"

Kelsey's door opened and a nurse rushed to her bedside.

"—minute," Deke finished.

"What is going on in here?" demanded the sturdy, middle-aged floor nurse dressed in pastel, purple- flowered scrubs with a hospital ID declaring her to be Linda Reath, R.N. While Linda took Kelsey's pulse, she kept shifting her accusatory glare between her watch and Deke's face.

"Sorry, Ma'am." Deke said. "We were talking about the accident and she got upset."

Kelsey tried to calm down, despite the series of upsetting anecdotes that Deke had just dumped into her hospital-gowned lap. This load of horse apples was going to take *a lot* more patience to wade through than her recently electrified mind could give it right now. When she felt better, she was going to kick ass and take names, but, for now, she needed to rest.

As Nurse Linda finished recording Kelsey's vitals in her online chart, she turned to Deke and pursed her lips. "I think it's time for visiting hours to be over now," the nurse's tone brooked no argument. "Ms. Taggert has suffered a severe shock to her system. She needs rest and to remain quiet while her system recovers."

Deke slowly rose from the chair and gently lifted Kelsey's limp hand. She felt the warmth of his hand sink into her bones and her tension began to relax. Just like at the accident site, she didn't want him to release her hand. "I'm sorry that I upset you. I'm sure there's an explanation. I'll look into it. As soon as I know anything, I'll give you a call." Deke placed her hand on the bed, patted it gently, and turned to leave. Again, Kelsey felt slightly bereft, but she was so tired and beginning to feel the pain that must have been managed by the magic i.v. in her arm creep back into every inch of her body, she could barely whisper, "How will you contact me? You don't have my phone number." Her earlier outburst had drained most of her energy reserves.

He winked. "I have my ways. If you learn all my secrets right away, you'll lose interest." He flashed a grin.

Kelsey's eyes widened in surprise at his blatant flirting. All she could do was stare as he strode to the door. "I'll be in touch." He lifted his hand in a small wave and left.

Nurse Linda sighed. "That is one good looking man. It's those eyes! They're so bright, they almost glow. What color do you think that is?"

"Key Lime Pie," replied Kelsey, letting loose a sigh of her own. Too bad he worked with her complete ass of an ex-husband. She would dearly love to have a taste of his Key Lime Pie.

Nurse Linda left with an admonishment to remain quiet, and to page her if she wanted anything to eat or drink. Kelsey started to rethink her position on mouth-wateringly tangy citrus desserts as the medication Nurse Linda injected into her i.v. began to kick in. A pleasurable sense of drowsiness seeped through her body. Pie.... Key Lime Pie. That's what she needed. Since her divorce—since two years before her divorce—she hadn't enjoyed pie.

Deke's face danced across her mental vision. Nurse Linda was right, those eyes... Kelsey released a relaxed sigh. A brush with death made a girl rethink her priorities. This last year, she'd thrown herself into her son and her work, forgetting about pie altogether. In fact, it was so long since she had had any pie, she'd almost forgotten the taste. Yeah, she mused as her limbs relaxed to cooked noodle consistency, Key Lime Pie was just what the doctor ordered.

CHAPTER THREE

Kelsey woke from a delicious dream to the rumbling of her stomach. It was uncanny timing, for at that very moment, her four friends pushed their way into the room carrying bags that wafted the heavenly scent of ...could it be? Dixie Chili! The aroma of spiced beef and hot dogs never failed to rouse Kelsey's appetite. Food from her favorite chili parlor was probably the one thing on earth that could have roused her appetite at this particular moment. She was still reeling from the ear bomb Deke had detonated, but for this childhood favorite comfort food, she would push through. Della dropped a bag with the red, white and blue logo from Newport, Kentucky's famous chili establishment onto Kelsey's wheeled bed tray table and then plunked down in the chair next to the bed. Kelsey raised the head of the bed, then gingerly opened the Styrofoam bowl containing her personal equivalent of manna from heaven. She tore open the accompanying single-serve baggies and began sprinkling on shredded cheddar cheese and oyster crackers.

"We only got a three-way," Della griped while pointing to

the pasta dish Kelsey was preparing to devour. "Cat and Jayne said beans and onions would be too much for your system to take right now. I lobbied hard for cheese coneys, but you only get two and only mustard...no onions there, either. Sorry!"

Lyssie and Cat crowded behind Della's chair. Jayne halted beside the bed and started unwrapping Kelsey's cheese coneys. Kelsey pushed the food around with the plastic fork. What had smelled so delicious a moment ago suddenly turned her stomach. She couldn't shake Deke's news.

"Thank you all so much, but I don't think I can eat. Suddenly, I don't feel very hungry." Kelsey looked at the spaghetti covered in chili and cheese and then looked away. "You guys feel free to dig in."

"What the hell is the matter with you?" demanded Cat. "You freaking LOVE this stuff! Did that shock change your DNA or something?"

Kelsey managed a wan smile , but her friends stared at her with a mixture of worry and suspicion. "Did that hulking knuckle-dragger upset you?" demanded Della. "I will kick his high, tight ass if he did something to put you off your food!"

Kelsey envisioned Deke's bitable backside. She shook her head slightly to banish the image of herself nipping his muscular butt cheek while she ran her hands up and down what she just *knew* would be muscular, fur-covered thighs. She *had* to stop thinking about the man like that!

"No, it was nothing Deke *did*. It was what he told me. None of you are going to *believe* this. My enormous Ex-Asshole just got himself *engaged*..and..that's not even the WORST PART! The delicious and eminently bitable Deke Connelly, who happens to be the co-owner and general contractor of the Mid-Life Crisis Mansion that the Shit Cannon is constructing for his new Botox Barbie was bought and paid for...in FULL...WITH CASH!

"Wait...WHAT?" Della sat bolt upright. Every one of her friends gasped breaths in utter disbelief.

"Yep! Apparently so," Kelsey snarled. "He has been jerking me around for MONTHS over child support, saying he hasn't gotten any commissions on car sales because the economy is so depressed. He's *obviously* lying through his bleached teeth and is probably doing something illegal to come up with that kind of cash! Now I just have to figure out what he's doing and how to bust his lying, cheating, skank-humping ass!"

Cat's face took on a calculating, lawyerly look. "Are you sure that he hasn't just been hiding money he made over the years? Could he be using money his parents gave him? I will have to do some research, but I believe that if Numb Nuts has hidden assets that he accumulated during your marriage, you are entitled to half of everything he put down on that house...which means, effectively, that you own part of the house. Better still, we may be able to sue him for misappropriating marital assets, and the court could impose punitive damages for fraud, leaving YOU the owner of the ENTIRE house, plus whatever other money that little pencil dick has been hiding."

"Holy Shit!" Jayne yelped. "Maybe we can repossess Barbie's brand new knockers. You know, from the front door." She made air quotes with her fingers.

They burst into hysterical giggles, but Kelsey was the first to sober up. "Girls, this is a big deal." Her smile faded she tensed her mouth as she looked each of her four soul sisters in the eye. "I don't want *anything* from that pathetic excuse for a penis carrier, but I will go to the ends of the earth to collect what belongs to my son. When he messed with our kid, he opened my whole *bag* full of crazy, and it's going to take a whole lot to close that bag back up."

"We are here for you, for whatever you need," Lyssie said,

while the other three nodded agreement. "For now, concentrate on getting out of here. After you're paroled, we'll come up with a game plan."

Kelsey dropped her head back onto her pathetically flat hospital pillow. "I am so disgusted. In a few days, I will be ready to kick ass and take names. I just want to make sure this doesn't hurt Charlie. He's disappointed enough that his dad skips the days together he promises him over and over. He need any more evidence the absolute ass-hat his dad really is."

She knew the outcome she wanted, but she didn't know how she was going to get there. She briefly closed her eyes and savored the idea of getting even with Brastard. The thought of watching that worm clean out his bank account and hand all the money over to her while Barbie looked on, pressing a tissue to her botoxed eyes, made Kelsey smile. The vision of Brad being carted away in handcuffs, sniveling like a little girl, made Kelsey's smile bigger. The mental vision of a prison guard with hands the size of a catcher's mitt performing a full cavity search on him made her positively giddy. But having to explain to Charlie that his dad was a conniving ass wiped that smile right off her face.

Jayne patted Kelsey's leg. "Kids know, Honey. They mostly keep up a front so we think we're doing a good job of protecting them. They work hard to protect their parents from knowing just how much they know. Anyway, we can plot Brad's downfall later. For now, let's destroy these coneys and three-ways. I have to pick the boys up from my mom's soon."

Feeling slightly more optimistic, Kelsey sat back up in her crummy hospital bed and dug into her fragrant spaghetti smothered in chili and cheese. She had taken only a few bites when it occurred to her that she had not called her parents or Charlie to let them know she was awake. "Can I borrow someone's phone? My cell phone didn't survive the *incident* and my room phone doesn't seem to work."

Lyssie handed her phone to Kelsey. "Take mine. I only use it for work calls, and I won't need it for a few days. The battery is charged, but if you're still here tomorrow, I'll bring the charger. The gallery isn't scheduled for any shows until next week. After you're discharged, I'll take you to get yours replaced and you can give mine back."

"Thanks, Lys." Kelsey smiled at her friend. "I need to call Charlie. He's probably worried."

Kelsey continued to chew while she dialed her parents' number. The call connected and rang once before her mother picked up. "Hello?"

"Hi, Mom. It's me. How are things going? Is Charlie okay?" Kelsey asked. "Oh, Kelsey, you're awake! Bill, Kelsey's awake! Thank God! I've been so worried. You were in and out when I left, but I didn't want to leave Charlie alone. I scared him when I rushed out of the house to come to you at the hospital, but I left him with your father in case it was bad. I didn't want him to see you until we knew more. What did the doctor say? When can you come home?" As a retired grade school teacher, it took a lot to rile Sheila Meyers, but apparently, having her only child struck by lightning had shaken her to the core.

"I'm doing okay...just tired, and my head's a little sore. The nurse said the doctor would be in soon and would tell us more. Is Charlie there? Can I talk to him?"

"Of course, Honey, just a second." Sheila's muffled voice called, "Charlie, come to the phone, Sweetie. Your mom wants to talk to you."

It only took a few seconds before Kelsey heard the boisterous voice of her six-year-old son, "Mommy! Is that you? Are you okay?" Kelsey had been proud of how well she had held herself together since learning about the accident, but hearing Charlie's voice cracked open the internal box that held all of her fear and anxiety. Her chest tightened with tears of relief upon hearing the precious voice, but she pulled up her "mom pants" and held herself together so she wouldn't scare her son.

"Hi, Little Man! It's me, all right. I'm doing just fine. I had a little accident yesterday during the storm and bumped my head, but I didn't even get stitches, so I am going to be fine!" Kelsey managed a warm, confident voice. No matter how bad she felt, she didn't want Charlie to worry any more than he had.

"Aw, Man. Not even a cast or nothin'? Why did you have stay there all night then? Do you even have your pajamas? I didn't, but Grandma got me some new Superman jammies at the store! Do you have any new super powers? I think Spiderman got his powers from being struck by lightning. Maybe you can fly now or something!" Charlie switched from one topic to the next at lightning speed, as only an excited six year old boy could. While he was supremely disappointed that his mom didn't have a cast, or even a good scab to show off, the thought of her having super powers certainly got him excited.

Kelsey laughed. The crazy excitement in Charlie's voice did wonders to loosen the ball of anxiety that had made her chest hurt. "No, Charlie, I don't think I can melt walls with my laser eyes, or even fly now. Sorry. I'm still just your mom. Are you being good for Grandma and Grandpa?"

"Yeah! I'm being so good, Grandpa says he is gonna tell Santa how good I am so I got some points stored up in case I do some bad stuff later. When are you gonna get here?" Charlie asked.

"I will probably be home tomorrow. I'll ask the doctor when he comes. Be good for Grandma and Grandpa, okay?"

"I will, Mommy! I'm gonna help Grandma make brownies

now. Bye!" Charlie's happy little voice faded as he handed the phone back to Kelsey's mom. She listened to his footfalls as he ran off, already hollering for his Grandpa.

"Honey, has the doctor told you anything about when you are going to be released yet?" Sheila asked. "Your dad and I can keep Charlie for as long as you need us and we can bring you right over here from the hospital if you need more time to recover."

"Thanks, Mom," Kelsey said as the doctor waltzed through her hospital room door. "The doctor just walked in. I'll call you back when I know more."

"Okay. Bye for now."

Kelsey pressed a button on the phone to end the call as Dr. Scott, the hospitalist assigned to her case, made his way over to her bed.

"So, young lady, hasn't anyone ever told you not to talk on the telephone during a thunderstorm?" Doctor Scott raised his eyebrows as he looked up from his tablet and over his half-lens glasses at her. "How are you feeling?"

"Like I've been flattened by a steamroller that I had to push off myself," Kelsey replied. "Unfortunately, the steam roller did *nothing* to flatten my flabby butt," she joked.

Dr. Scott did not laugh. He didn't even smirk. Apparently, he did not joke about near-death experiences *or* fat backsides.

"Lingering muscle soreness and fatigue is common after an electric shock. All of your muscles, including your heart, constrict when that type of energy hits your system. As a standard procedure, we're keeping you hooked up to a heart monitor for twenty-four hours to make sure your heart's electric rhythm isn't misfiring. If you continue to show a reliable heart rhythm and no other symptoms, we can release you tomorrow. Any questions?" The doctor looked up her electronic medical chart and met her gaze.

"Was I really struck by lightning? Shouldn't I have burns or something?" Kelsey asked.

Doctor Scott said, "From the description the paramedics gave, you were lying very near a burned patch of earth. They made the assumption, based on their experience and the eyewitness's description, that the lightning must have struck the ground. The best we can determine is that the strike hit your cell phone and jolted you pretty good before you let go. The whole thing probably lasted a fraction of a second...literally the time it would take you to blink. You don't have an entry or exit burn, so I surmise that your phone took the brunt of the electricity and you were grounded by your rubber shoes. You are a very, very lucky lady." The doctor finally smiled, waived at her friends, and left to see his next patient.

As the doctor's explanation sank in, Kelsey thought hard about what a difference a second could make. *If* she hadn't slowed her stride just enough to try to call Brad or *if* she had worn her cute kitten heals instead of her rubber-soled, faux cork platform wedges... And Cinderella thought *her* shoes were lucky. "Wow." Kelsey exhaled a long, slow breath and repeated, "Just...WOW."

Della, always the first to lighten a heavy mood, quipped, "Kels, the first thing you gotta do when you are discharged is buy a lottery ticket. You are on fire! Well, you're *electrifying*....get it? Electrifying?" As the rest of the ladies made derogatory noises, she said, "C'mon! You know that was funny! Too soon?"

Kelsey laughed, just a little, mostly at Della's antics rather than at her joke. "What would I do without you girls?" Kelsey wondered aloud.

"Well," Cat surmised, "your life would certainly lack a whole lotta awesome!" All of the ladies laughed as they gathered their purses and quickly said their goodbyes. They promised to visit tomorrow if she was still at the hospital, or to check in on Kelsey if she went home.

"Thanks for everything. I am really tired all of a sudden. I think I'll sleep." Kelsey lowered the head of the bed and closed her eyes as her room emptied of visitors. Not surprisingly, her stubborn mind drifted to thoughts of the hunky contractor feeding her Key Lime Pie....

CHAPTER FOUR

Later that afternoon, Deke picked up some last-minute supplies at the local builders' supply, still mulling over his conversation with Kelsey. Knowing that telling her about her ex's house financials had made a bad situation worse tore him up. He needed to hear someone he trusted tell him he wasn't the jackass he thought he was. Deke finished up his self-checkout and maneuvered the dolly full of two by fours and hardware out of the store. Deke continued across the busy parking lot and hit the unlock button on his key fob before opening the door to his black Ford F-150 Super Duty pickup truck. After quickly loading everything into the extended truck bed, Deke closed the lift gate, returned the dolly to the cart wrangling area and pulled his phone from the belt holster he had clipped to his Wranglers. Deke punched redial on Eli Yates' cell number He waited for his long-time friend and co-owner to pick up while he walked back to his truck and climbed up into the driver's seat.

Eli picked up on the first ring. "Hey, Man! What's up?"

"I'm just leaving the builders supply. I'm running a little

late getting this extra lumber to the site. I went to check on the woman who was hurt yesterday at The Retreat site."

"How's she doing? Did you find out why she was unaccompanied at our building site?" Eli asked.

"She's going to be okay," Deke said. "Apparently, she's Brad Taggert's ex-wife. She was trying to catch up with him to give him hell because he stood up their kid to do the freaky cleansing ritual with Voodoo Barbie."

Deke and Eli shared a short laugh at the nickname they had given Brad's fiancée, Barbie Delacroix. Neither man had much patience for crazy women, and Barbie's more "obvious" assets, proudly displayed in some low-cut blouse or sweater, were more than overshadowed by her abrasive personality and her annoying habit of changing their building plans based on her daily horoscope and "messages" she received from her "Spiritual Advisor, Khan." He laid his head against the leather headrest and sighed. They put up with a lot as custom home builders. They had built their company's reputation on giving their clients *exactly* what they asked for, within budget and on time. Their clients were generally wealthy, demanding people, which was to be expected when the average home they build cost one and a half million dollars. Brad and Barbie were a *whole* other category of demanding, though. There wasn't a single room in the original home plan that Barbie hadn't wanted to tweak. She called it "Spiritual Optimization," but Deke and Eli called it infuriating.

"Happy to hear she's going to be okay," Eli's voice interrupted his thoughts and brought him back to the conversation at hand. "I was concerned we'd have a lawsuit *and* some government agency all over us if she was injured on our property during a surprise inspection."

Deke fiddled with the buckle of the tool belt on the passenger seat . "Well," he warned, "we might not be out of the woods yet." Deke tried to decide how much to say.

"What do you mean? I thought you said the chick was fine."

"Her name is Kelsey," Deke snapped before he caught himself. "She'll recover from her physical injuries. I'm just not so sure she'll get over the brick I dropped on her while making small talk."

"What did you say, Deke?" Eli's question came back heavy with dread.

"When she told me she went to the site to catch up with her deadbeat ex who hadn't paid child support in five months, I got upset." Deke ran his hand through his hair. "I *might* have blurted out that Taggert paid cash for the build." Deke closed his eyes. Instead of the angry reply he expected, Deke heard an incredibly long sigh and then, "I don't even know what to say, Man. I don't think the information's confidential, but *Brad Taggert* is our client, not this Kelsey woman, and he has every right to expect us to be discreet. Hell, she might have been lying. She could be just as crazy as that chick he's seeing now. God knows, his taste seems to run to crazy."

Deke's anger spiked at hearing Eli's accusation. Unlike Eli, he'd met Kelsey...talked to her. He knew she was telling the truth.

"Just to be safe, I think we better call our lawyer and make sure we aren't liable for giving out that kind of information."

"I agree. And while we've got the lawyer on the phone, ask if we can get into trouble for helping Kelsey build a case for getting some of the child support Taggert owes her. Assholes like him give all men a bad name. If he can afford granite countertops and custom made cabinetry, he can afford to help pay for his kid."

"Slow down, Deke," Eli said. "We don't know if this Kelsey chick was telling the truth. I mean, I think Taggert is a douche, but we don't have any proof that he's a deadbeat dad."

Deke looked at his reflection in the rear-view mirror and saw a look of determination staring back at him. "Damn it, Eli, I told you not to call her a chick! I know Kelsey is telling the truth. Don't ask me how, I just know. I can't explain why, but I have to help her."

Eli mumbled, "Sorry, Man. Since when do you get pissed at me for calling some woman you barely know a chick?"

Eli's question stopped Deke cold. Since when *did* he get so irritated by a friend's passing remark? Something about Kelsey made him want to protect her. Maybe it was some weird reaction to saving her life, but Kelsey Taggert had become *important* to him...very important.

After a short silence, Eli startled Deke by snorting loudly into the phone. "Huh! I know *exactly* why!" Eli said. "She's hot and you want to get into her pants!"

Deke started to tell Eli that he was dead wrong, but he couldn't. "I don't just want to get into her pants, Man. She isn't that kind of lady. She's beautiful and she's classy. I just hate to see her struggling because of some rich, tightwad asshole."

"Sure. I got it," Eli said. "I just hope your rescue mission doesn't land our company in a pile of shit."

"Just talk to the lawyer. See what our options are so I can make sure my slipup produces the least amount of compost possible." Deke inserted the key in the ignition. "I gotta go. See you tomorrow at the site."

"Later." Eli hung up.

Deke ended the call and wondered how he could help Kelsey Taggert and her little boy without screwing up his company's hard-earned reputation for great customer service.

A thought occurred to him as he turned the key in the ignition. He and Eli had been talking about getting an assistant to help with paperwork and filing. For six years, they'd been doing everything themselves, but with their increased success came a backlog of paperwork cluttering the C&Y Construction office. They could use a snazzy new website, too, and Deke knew *just* the sexy little blue-eyed brunette web designer and virtual assistant to help them. If he just *happened* to get the lady to spend a little quality time with him during the process, well, all that much better! Deke put the truck in drive and started whistling as he drove toward his building site.

CHAPTER FIVE

Kelsey passed the week of her recovery touring three of Dante's nine circles of hell, all from the comfort of her parents' guest room. She didn't know which had been worse, the Knitting a Scarf Circle, the Mother-Approved Bodice-Ripping Virginity-Losing Romance Novel Reading Circle, or the dreaded Spider Solitaire on her dad's tablet computer Circle of Hell. She was officially stir-crazy. Her body now hummed along at its usual level of nervous energy, confirming that she'd finally recovered from her little run-in with Mother Nature. All of her fingers and toes were crossed in the hope that her family doctor would release her with a clean bill of health at today's check-up.

Every day she spent trying to keep her injured body quiet enough to recover from her physical injuries ensured that her business and her overactive mind slipped further into chaos. Being self-employed provided a lot of flexibility, and Kelsey had managed to surreptitiously work on a few web-design projects while she was supposed to be napping in her old twin-sized bed. These sporadic work sessions were barely enough to keep clients from thinking she had fallen off the face of the earth. She needed to get back to her house and her equipment in order to ramp up to her normal level of efficiency and to jump back on top of the projects waiting for her special touch.

Kelsey wasn't just anxious to get back to spreadsheets and payroll tax calculations, though. Coming so close to death had prompted her to take a good long look at her whole life... her whole, entire, thoroughly scheduled, organized, boring, predictable life. She and the girls used to raise hell. Now all she raised was a kid and a kitchen herb garden that she rarely remembered to water. During their college days, the five of them were known across campus for knowing how to have fun without getting caught. They were legends in their own minds. They had kept their Girls' Night Out tradition going strong, long after they had left college in their rear view mirrors, but Kelsey had been making excuses and missing out on the fun way to often lately. When was the last time she had managed a well-deserved hangover after staying out too late laughing and drinking with the girls? Kelsey couldn't recall the last time her whole body surged with adrenaline from trying something scary, or laughed so hard she'd almost wet herself, or scared herself spitless watching a horror movie.

It hit Kelsey, in that moment, that she had been merely existing in her life she and Brad had tied the knot after college, not really *living*. For the last few years of marriage, she focused on taking care of Charlie and building her business to supplement the meager and inconsistent income that Brad earned at his various jobs. She had become a stick-in-the-mud. Since her divorce, she had been struggling to make a life for herself and her son that would make Charlie happy and fulfilled, but she had barely peeked her head out of her front door. Friends and family got lost in the daily scramble, and "dating" was a word she'd have to look up in a dictionary.

Her body might be recovering from her accident, but her social life remained on life support. What she needed was a Social Life Defibrillator...a great big shock to her comatose Party Hearty. She was not even forty years old, damn it! It was time she started living life instead of existing.

At the end of the day, Kelsey *hated* that her marriage had ended in divorce. She had fought for so long to keep Brad's interest that she couldn't remember what it felt like to be unconditionally loved by a member of the opposite sex...one not related to her. Brad leaving her for Trailer Tramp Barbie had actually been a real life-upgrade for Kelsey. Now that she wasn't worrying about making more money than Brad and keeping his fragile ego from being damaged by her success, she enjoyed her work a lot more. She was excellent at doing her job and prided herself on finishing ahead of schedule. Her clients were thrilled with her work and generous in referring new clients, so Kelsey's business had grown at a rapid pace. When she finished a project, she always a new challenge waiting in her inbox, so she jumped right into the next client file. When she wasn't working, she was helping Charlie with his homework or doing laundry or working in her little cottage garden. Life as Kelsey the Single Mom/Small Business Owner/Homeowner kept her busy, but she needed to remember that Kelsey the Woman needed tending, too. After all, if she didn't balance her life, soon enough she was going to burn out. Prying herself away from her laptop was the place to start. She needed to learn how to have a social life.

When in doubt, Kelsey always made a list. Putting things in writing helped her focus and problem solve. Her problem was that she was in a rut. What better way to get out of a rut than to make a list of things to do to change up her same-old, same-old. What she needed was a Bucket List! They didn't have to be huge things, like skydiving. They could be small, like learning how to grow vegetables from seed or changing her motor oil. The sky, budgetarily limited to her conservative savings account, was the limit, and she certainly had plenty of time to think about it this week. The biggest challenge was *what* to include on her list.

Where to start...where to start...Kelsey tapped her pencil against her chin and considered all the possibilities. By the ripe old age of thirty-nine, most of her friends had already experienced some pretty exciting life experiences. Kelsey recalled all the fabulous adventure stories other people had bragged about over the years. Race Car Driving? Excellent endorphin rush...but she didn't really care about driving fast. Sky Diving? Endorphin typhoon, but Kelsey had never liked heights. Scuba Diving? Really interesting, but not much to look at in the local gravel quarry where her friends had taken scuba diving lessons while she was pregnant with Charlie. Kelsey decided to table that one until she could head to a tropical location with beautiful underwater sights. She had no trouble coming up with great ideas for big adventures, and they all sounded Bucket List Worthy. The problem was that the shine on all of these activities began to dim when Kelsey couldn't think of anyone who could go with her. Maybe she should start with solitary activities.... What would she be perfectly happy doing all by herself?

Kelsey snorted. She was really tired of doing *one thing* completely by herself. Even with the new fantasy fodder provided by Deke, the Plaid Clad God of Home Building this week, Kelsey still missed the feel of an actual human being touching her. She didn't need or want another selfish, whiny man in her life, but she definitely missed sex. While Brad had never set their sheets on fire, he had been a very sexual man in the early years of their relationship. Her sex life definitely petered out after Charlie's birth, but Brad had still sought her out in the middle of the night, right up until he left her for the business-trip-to-Vegas bimbo. Of all the endorphin rushing experiences that other people had described, Kelsey felt the most envy about other women's tales of fantastic sex.

Hmmm, Kelsey thought, maybe *SEX* is the perfect place to start! She knew this would involve dating, or at least, trolling for men, but she didn't want the emotional entanglements that led to marrying selfish assholes, so she had to approach this like every single man seemed to: no strings attached passion. Hit it and Quit it. Not quite one night stands...more of a Friend with Benefits situation...Netflix and Chill as the hipsters called it. According to all of the women's magazines at the grocery store check-out line, tons of guys probably dreamed of a woman who wanted nothing more than a little mutual satisfaction. She could do this!

Plenty of men out there only wanted a quick hookup with a woman, especially a woman who was more than willing to pay for her own dinner. She was pretty certain she could find someone to help her with her newly percolating sex drive. In fact, she might even *have* the perfect candidate. Since learning the name of her rescuer and being on the receiving end of his teasing flirtation, Kelsey couldn't stop fantasizing about getting Deke into bed...or onto a couch....or in an empty field.....or onto a beach somewhere, and stripping him naked. She hadn't thought so much about sex since she'd hit puberty. Now, after twelve years of mediocre sex, she knew what she was missing. Deke was a definite possibility for her first no-strings-attached fling.

It was high time she owned her womanhood and learned how to have good, *mind*-blowing sex without having to do laundry and make someone a sandwich afterwards. After all, women reached their sexual peak in their forties and Kelsey would be forty in three months. Kelsey and her single-again friends were all looking for a worthy man to help them scale that peak, so to speak. It was hard to find a good man to date when you were divorced and raising a son. According to the magazine articles she'd had time to read in the *really long* check-out lines, behind the extreme couponers and the retirees from the assisted living facility that bought their groceries with rolls of coins, it was *really* hard to find a quality date when you were over forty. But Kelsey knew that she had a slight advantage over most women her age because she didn't really want a permanent relationship.

Her marriage had given her enough experience with "relationships" to last her a lifetime. She just wanted to have sex... lots of good sex. She figured the unicorn of true love was permanently grazing in someone else's pasture. She could, however, believe in finding true lust, especially with a certain heroic contractor who resembled Hollywood's version of a mythical Norse God.

Over the years, Kelsey had gone through periods of vague discontent when she felt like something was lacking in her marriage, like she and Brad had lost all the youthful passion that had driven their intimacy. What it boiled down to was that her marriage had no spark. The spontaneous lovemaking that she and Brad had enjoyed at the beginning of their relationship had given way to weeks of trying to get a full night's sleep after Charlie had been born. Instead of embracing fatherhood, Bard had seemed to view Charlie as a challenge to his importance in their marriage. He constantly complained that Kelsey never made time for him anymore and when Charlie was only months old, he went back to the Community Theater group, spending less and less time at home.

Being the mother of a baby was tiring, but being a wife to Brad was *exhausting.* The stress of raising a family while trying to keep food on the table while Brad frittered away his mediocre paychecks on voice lessons and acting workshops had worn Kelsey's love down to nothing. By the last year of their marriage, she didn't even have enough give-a-damn to fight with him about it. Since there was no fighting, their formerly passionate make-up sex never really happened anymore, either.

Kelsey killed a few hours in her old bedroom closet, looking through her college scrapbooks and admiring the fierce girl that she had been. She had loved dressing in next to nothing and sneaking into clubs with her badly forged fake I.D. She had danced to club music and drunk cheap draft beer with until the clubs kicked her and her best friends out. When the clubs closed, they piled into their old beater cars and drove to some all-night greasy spoon to eat French fries until their stomachs had soaked up all of that night's alcohol, then they headed to bed, only to get a few hours sleep, head to class and do it all over again the next night.

Fifteen years and one kid later, Kelsey was *still* fierce, but today's ferocity was not founded in her childlike belief that she was invincible. Kelsey 2.0 was fierce because she had survived the worst that she had imagined life could throw at her and she was still standing strong.

Kelsey knew that she wasn't bad looking and that she still had a damned fine rack for someone pushing 40 who had breastfed a child. She had a steady stream of business based on word-of-mouth referrals and she could demand top dollar for her time. She had a nice little house that she had bought for herself, a new car and a fantastic group of friends and family. She had almost everything she wanted from life. The only thing she really missed was someone to warm her bed. She didn't need to look any further than Deacon Connelly. She just had to figure out a way to ask him out that didn't make him think she was after anything other than a good time.

Before she could dive into what she hoped would be a torrid sex affair, though, Kelsey knew she needed to finally put her failed marriage to rest by finding out where Brad had gotten so much cash and why he was keeping it from Charlie. She had been racking her brain to figure out where Brad could have gotten so much money. There was no way that she could have missed a million dollars in cash that Brad had earned from any of the many jobs he had bounced between while they were married. Hell, most weeks he shoved his pathetic paycheck at her on the way out the door because he was "too busy" to go to the bank. God, what a prick!

Late on Wednesday afternoon, Kelsey was washing dishes in her mom's quaint 1950's kitchen when she heard a quick series of raps on the side door next to the sink. She leaned to the left, hands still immersed in soapy water and smiled at her friend Cat who was peering through the glass."Get in here!" she laughed. "You know you don't have to knock!"

Cat opened the door and strolled into the kitchen, lugging her briefcase and a cardboard take-out drink holder filled with magical white paper cups with steam seeping from the lids.

"I see your Mom still hasn't popped for a dishwasher, huh?" Cat remarked, unloading her bag and the drinks onto the kitchen dinette set.

"Why should she?" Kelsey retorted. "She has Dad to do the dishes!" Both women laughed. Kelsey dried her hands and joined Cat at the kitchen table. "What temptation have you brought?"

"Well, since I come bearing bad news, I thought that I had also better come bearing gifts." Cat looked up at Kelsey and pursed her lips.

"Uh oh," Kelsey said. "I know that look. Just let me have it."

Cat handed Kelsey one of the cups and said, "Here. Take a big drink of this first. Then I will tell you what my research showed."

Kelsey inhaled the delicious vanilla coffee scent wafting

toward her nose and took a sip. Sighing deeply, she looked Cat directly in the eye.

"Okay...Hit me."

Cat sighed just as deeply as Kelsey had just done. "You're going to have to re-open your divorce."

Kelsey's whole body tensed instantly and the coffee that had just gone down so smoothly threatened to come right back up again.

"What?" she questioned her oldest friend. "How can this be the only option?"

"It's not the only option, Kelsey, but it is the best one." Cat stated. Kelsey heard the certainty in Cat's voice. Her friend would never try to convince her that this was the best option if she truly didn't believe it.

"Okay. Why?" Kelsey tried to relax her suddenly knotted neck muscles by rubbing them with her hand that was still warm from gripping her coffee cup. It wasn't enough. She wavered between trying to listen to Cat and wondering where her dad kept the whiskey. She was going to need a little Irish in her coffee to get through this conversation. Cat started to explain that, while it was unusual to reopen a divorce in court, her research had dug up legal precedent that proved it could be done when you could show that your former spouse had neglected to mention certain assets to the court as part of the divorce proceedings. Since Kelsey didn't know where to start looking, Cat suggested that she hire a forensic accountant to look into Brad's financial and credit history. If Brad had come into money while they were married that he had hidden from her, Kelsey could sue him for equitable distribution and get her share, even though their divorce was final. Cat also said that if Brad had hidden the money in anticipation of divorcing her, she could even get punitive damages and end up with ALL of the money at issue. While she didn't relish spending any more of her life on the waste of human skin that was Brad Taggert, she could NOT let him get away with stealing from her son!

Kelsey had spent her life avoiding conflict. She was notorious for being the peacemaker of their social group, but even peaceful people had their breaking points. She was definitely ready for this battle. After finishing her coffee and deciding to take her friend's advice, Kelsey gave Cat a one dollar retainer (since that is all Cat would take) and told her to go ahead and petition the court to re-open her divorce proceedings. While it was risky tipping her hand before she had actual proof, Cat had mentioned that the court would scrutinize all of Brad's finances during the proceedings, which might keep him from wasting any more money that should go to Charlie. Cat had already prepared all of the paperwork before she stopped by for Kelsey's signature and she took it all to the courthouse to file before the ink on her signature was even dry. After stopping at the courthouse to get the County Clerk's file stamp, Cat told her she planned to drop a copy of the filing at Brad's attorney's office. She could have sent a runner from her office, but Cat like to look her opponents in the eye and see the fear on their faces when they saw her coming through the door. She was *that* much of a legend in the local legal community! Cat figured that Brad's attorney would contact him right away, so the shit should be hitting the fan any day now.

After starting the legal work to re-open her divorce on Wednesday, the rest of the week flew by. When Friday rolled around, she had an appointment with her family doctor to see if she was fit to return to work...and her own home. As she put the finishing touches on her makeup, her shiny new cell phone launched into "Thunderstruck" by AC/DC....apparently, her friends' idea of a funny ring-tone. They must have re-programmed her phone while one of them distracted her with chocolate during their sick room sit-ins this week. That's what she got for using the same PIN number for every account she owned. The caller I.D. said "private caller" so she tamped down her urge to answer, "Welcome to the Thunder Dome, "and just said, "Hello?"

"Kelsey? Is that you?" a familiar voice whined. Kelsey scrunched up her face in distaste. Brad didn't let her answer before he started in on his inquisition. "Why did my lawyer call me this morning and tell me that you are re-opening our divorce? I mean, I'm sorry that I didn't pick Charles up this weekend, but we had a real situation on our hands at the house and Barbie didn't think it was safe, you know, *spiritually,* for a child to be present. It was for his own safety. I promise I will take him this weekend. There is no need to get our lawyers involved." Brad finished with a dramatic exhale.

Kelsey removed the phone from her ear and thought about hanging up. She counted to three and moved the phone back toward her head. She spoke in the calm, stilted tone she reserved for any annoying person, "First, Bradley, our son hates being called by his full name as much as you do, which you would know if you spent more than five minutes a month with him. Second, I am not re-opening our divorce to try to incentivize you to spend time with our son. You should want to do that because *you are his father*, not because a judge orders you to! I am reopening our divorce because my accountant brought some financial irregularities to my attention. Since it appears there were some misstatements of income during our divorce proceedings, I will be asking the judge to re-examine our financial settlements." Kelsey was very careful to not specify *which* statements were problematic. Since he was such an egomaniac, she knew he would assume that the mistake had been hers.

"Our financial settlement? Why?" Brad asked in a shocked tone. "Is this about the child support? I told you I would pay everything as soon as my annual sales bonus came through. I'm just strapped for cash until then," he whined.

Cat and Kelsey had discussed how to handle the questions Brad was bound to ask without tipping their hand. Cat had recommended the old IRS defense.

"I received an inquiry from the IRS asking for clarification on our last joint tax return. Apparently, something we filed raised a red flag," Kelsey intoned in her best innocent and confused, yet ignorant and trusting voice. "I'm sure it's nothing, but since you have all the records for the last few years of our marriage, we have to go through the official channels to keep all of this above-board. You know...to avoid an audit."

"Well, right, I guess," Brad stumbled. Kelsey could tell that mentioning the IRS had shaken him. "Right, then, I will, uh, just see what I need to do...." Brad's voice faded away.

"Since you weren't able to include Charlie in your activities last weekend, I'm sure that you and Barbie have planned something really fun for him this weekend to make it up to him. Just give me a call when you firm up your plans. Goodbye, Brad." Kelsey hit the end button while murmuring, "Asshole....no, ass-half. It would take two of you to make a whole ass."

She headed out to the foyer to meet her mom and head to the doctor's office. Let the Games Begin. Brad would start scrambling to cover his "assets" if he got even a *hint* that she was onto his fraud. She hoped to get her "get out of jail free card" from the doctor and be ready to *really* look into the situation with Brad and his hidden stash of cash

Kelsey bent over a clipboard, updating her medical insurance information, when the familiar rumbling of a certain God of

Mischief's deep voice next to her right ear caused her to jump and drop her pen.

"Would it *shock you* to know that I have been thinking about you?" Deke Connelly looked at Kelsey with a mischievous glint in his eyes. His lips twitched like he was trying to keep from grinning at his outrageously bad joke "What? Too soon for the electric shock jokes?" he asked, innocently. The object of all of her recent fantasies was standing next to her chair, holding one bandaged hand close to his chest, the other holding the front door of the doctor's office that he had just come through.

Kelsey's hand flew to her chest to calm her jumping pulse, which was not entirely caused by Deke's surprise appearance. "The only thing shocking here is your sense of humor!" Kelsey said with a laugh. "How long have you been waiting to use that?"

"Kelsey, do you want to introduce me to your friend?" her mom asked from the seat next to hers.

Deke held out a giant calloused hand. "Hello, Ma'am. I'm Deke Connelly."

Kelsey piped in with, "Mom, this was the man who called 911 when the lightning hit me. Kelsey purposefully didn't mentioned that the man who saved her life was also the contractor building her ex-husband's new house.

Kelsey's mom gasped, stood up, and pulled Deke in for a hug. Deke moved his injured hand away from his body just in time to avoid getting it smashed. He looked a little surprised, but let Sheila squeeze him without protest. Sheila released him from the hug, and leaned back to look up into his face as she grasped his hand with both of hers. "Oh my God, it's you! I can't even *tell* you how grateful I am, I am so grateful! I'm Sheila Meyers, Kelsey's mom. Her dad and I want to thank you so much for what you did to help our little girl." Sheila's eyes filled with tears as she continued, "If you hadn't been there, I don't know what would have happened to her." Sheila's lip started to tremble and Deke patted her shoulder awkwardly with his bandaged hand while Kelsey looked on in affectionate embarrassment.

"Mom! Stop! I'm fine," Kelsey said, wanting to calm her mother's anxiety.

"Mrs. Meyers, I didn't do anything anybody else wouldn't have done. There is no need to thank me," Deke said while trying to extricate his hand from her sniffling mother's grasp. His eyes pleaded with Kelsey for help in freeing himself. Kelsey smiled, getting a bit of a charge out of the fact that it was Deke in the uncomfortable position this time. "What are you doing here, Deke?"

Deke waived his bandaged left hand, showing white gauze taped across the palm. "I got hit with a nail from the pneumatic nail gun last week and had to have a few stitches. Doc Grainger's removing the stitches today. My palm has been itchy, and now I'm beginning to believe in that ancient Chinese saying about itchy palms meaning good luck." Deke smiled at Kelsey with a sexy gleam in his eye.

Kelsey looked into Deke's beautiful light green eyes and started to heat up. "Oh?" she asked in a slightly breathless voice. "I thought itchy palms meant money was coming your way."

Deke grinned."I like my version better. Anyway, I have been meaning to call you, but this week got crazy. I have that research I promised to do. Also, I talked to my partner Eli about your business and I was hoping you could help us out. Our website is one of those "design it yourself" jobs off the internet and we want to upgrade our online image. Plus, we could really use some help organizing all the paperwork around the office. We should set up a time to get together and talk...you know, kill two birds with one stone. Do you have a card?"

"Here," her mom interrupted, pressing a card into Deke's uninjured hand. Deke put the card into his front pocket and caught Kelsey's eye. She had been staring intently at his face. Her eyes darted away quickly, but she felt her cheeks heat from embarrassment at being caught staring. He was just so damned pretty! The door to the exam rooms opened, startling Kelsey's attention away from her perusal of Deke's "pocket." He winked at her and said, "I'll be in touch. Mrs. Meyers, it was nice to meet you."

"You, too, Deke!" Sheila grinned at him as the nurse called Kelsey's name. Kelsey and her mom followed the nurse into the inner sanctum of the doctor's office.

The door to the waiting room had barely swished closed when Sheila started in on her daughter."Kelsey," Sheila admonished loudly, "you didn't tell me he was so good looking!"

"Mom," Kelsey hissed, "he can hear you."

"Good! I hope he hears me say that I bet he calls you!" Sheila and the nurse laughed at Kelsey's blush as they walked back into one of Doctor Grainger's examination rooms.

Too bad that all Deke wanted was her professional help.

Suddenly, a little light bulb went on in her brain. She *could* kill two birds with one stone. Working on Deke's website would give her an opportunity to feel him out about a potential love affair...and helping C&Y Construction could be the ticket she needed to get more information on Brad's financial arrangements. Even if the records don't track the cash deposit Deke had mentioned, at least it gave her a place to start. Cat was pretty sure that, wherever Brad had gotten the money, he had probably sheltered it in Bimbo Barbie's name.

If Deke didn't call her, Kelsey vowed right then and there to call him herself and offer her services as a "thank you" for what he had done. Even if she had to work for free, Kelsey *had* to get into that office. If she happened to mention, in passing, her need for a Bucket List companion, she could gauge his reaction to her offer of naked companionship.

Hopefully, she would have an opportunity to see the paperwork on Brad and Barbie's house. Maybe she could explain to Deke what she needed. At the hospital, he had certainly seemed sympathetic to her plight. All she could do was ask, even if it meant that Deke would see her as a victim and not the sexy, independent business woman computer nerd...no, scratch that—not a nerd; she was an Intellectual Bad Ass—that he might want to see naked. If he didn't want the naked part, at least she would have a head start on building a secure future for her son. Charlie came first, but she was beginning to see her way to making herself a close second.

Deke wasn't in the waiting room when Kelsey finished up with Doctor Grainger. If he remained in the building, he'd probably heard the whoop of joy she'd given when the doctor had pronounced her fully recovered. Nothing could ruin her mood today! She was a Free Woman! She would call him tomorrow. Right now, she had to get with The Girls, celebrate her freedom with a drink, and plan Operation Repo Barbie's Dream House.

CHAPTER SIX

That night the girls met Kelsey at her house with red wine, chocolate cake and an extra large pizza smothered in cheese and sausage to celebrate her escape from Parent Prison. They raised a toast to whatever higher power had put Deke Connelly in the right place at the right time to save Kelsey's life. Kelsey made her own toast to good friends, good wine and a good life, ending with, "Cheers to still having my life to live, and to living the hell out of the time I have left!"

"Here, here!" the girls chorused and then drank.

"Kelsey, I have been thinking," started Lyssie, "and I have decided that you are not the only one who has been coasting through life lately, not really living every day to the fullest. I mean, I wouldn't have wished what happened to you on anyone, but your brush with death has made me reconsider my life."

Cat jumped in, "Me, too! I love all of you and I love my job, but what in the hell are five hot, successful, intelligent women doing sitting around their friend's kitchen eating pizza on a Friday night? We should be out, tearing up the town!"

"Remember how we used to spend most of the week looking forward to Friday night?" Jayne asked. "When we were younger, we waited for the weekend so we could stop being boring and responsible and cut loose. Now, all I do on Friday night is make a list of all of the crap I have to get done by Sunday so that the next boring week will be just as boring as the week before." Jayne sighed and took another drink of wine. Kelsey and Cat nodded their heads enthusiastically in agreement and took healthy sips of their cabernet. Lyssie sat swirling the wine in the bottom of her glass with a faraway look on her face.

Della poked the half-eaten slice of pizza on her plate. "When did we all get so *old?*" she asked.

The women fell silent, none of them answering the question.

Kelsey set her wine glass on the table with a bang loud enough to get everyone's attention. "Well, I, for one, am *not* going to live like that anymore!" she declared. "I have done nothing for the past week but think about what has been and what could have been. I am sick to fucking death of thinking about the past. I want to start looking forward to the future!" Kelsey raised her glass and took another large sip of the fruity red wine.

"Me, too!" Della agreed. "We are vibrant, interesting, good-looking women who work hard. We deserve to play hard, too. I, for one, am sick to death of dating my vibrator. We have spent so much time together, I finally had to give him a name."

Cat snorted. "You mean, B.O.B., for Battery Operated Boyfriend?"

"No, actually, I named him Manuel," Della said, "because he'd done the job as *well* as any *man* I have been with, up till now." All of the girls burst into hysterical laughter, fueled in no small part by their wine consumption.

"I love my vibrator," sighed Jayne, "but I miss the weight of a man laying over me while making love. I miss having something warm to cuddle up with at night."

"Well, I've got a big, spoiled dog that takes up more than his fair share of my bed," quipped Cat, "but I really miss the companionship, too. There really is something to be said for having someone to talk to after sex." Cat swirled the remaining wine in the bottom of her glass and watched it intently.

Lyssie smacked her palm down on the table. "Enough of this moping. If we are the intelligent, sexy, savvy women we claim to be, then we should start going after the kind of life we want. We deserve it.

"That's it, Ladies," Kelsey declared. "We have reached our sexual peak, and we are not getting any younger. We deserve to enjoy all that our lives and our bodies have to offer. All we need is the appropriate tool to get the job done. We all need a man!" Kelsey thrust her finger in the air for emphasis.

Della got a mulish look on her face and said, "I don't *need* a man for anything. I have been just fine on my own for years, and I don't see that changing."

"Oh, stop it, Della! Who are you trying to convince?" Lyssie demanded. "You cannot live the rest of your life alone and be happy. You loved Dave, and I know that losing him was a terrible blow, but you are too young to give up on love."

"We are *all* too young to give up," Jayne said. "In fact, let's make a pact to try to find someone special." She looked hopefully around at her companions. Each wore a different expression, ranging from hopeful to pessimistic, but none of them said no.

"Who is with me?" Jayne asked, putting her hand, palm down, in the middle of the table. "Come on!"

One by one, the girls added their hands to the pile.

"Good!" declared Jayne. "Now, what we need is a plan. Where can we find good looking, financially stable single men to have wild monkey sex with?" She finished with a laugh.

Lyssie piped in, "Well, I don't know about where the rest of us can look, but I know exactly who Kelsey's first candidate should be.....that delicious hunk of hero that saved her life. Deke Connelly!"

"Oh my god, yes!" Cat said. "He is perfect, and he already has the hots for you, Kelsey!"

"I don't know about that," Kelsey demurred, "but he is absolutely delicious. I wouldn't mind jumping back into the dating pool if he were swimming around in it."

"Preferably naked," Lyssie cooed.

"Amen!" The girls clinked glasses.

The girls heartily approved Kelsey's intention to get her groove on and they brainstormed the best way to approach Delicious Deke about getting together for a little one-on-one, naked, four-square action. They all agreed it was a brilliant first move to offer her professional services to Deke's construction company, *especially* if she made an exception and worked in the C&Y offices instead of her home office, as she typically did. She'd have a lot more opportunities to feel Deke out about a possible dating relationship without appearing too forward. She could certainly justify her change in typical "virtual assistance" policy since they were local, unlike the rest of her other clients which were scattered across the country. Deke had mentioned needing help sorting their records, so she would probably have to be on-site at their offices...it only made sense. *Wink, wink.*

"You know what else?" Cat piped in. "If you work in their offices, you might be able to get a look at Brad and Boob's building contract. If there is anything in there about how they paid for the house or where the cash actually came from, you could save yourself a lot of time and money on the forensic accountant."

Della pointed out that she would have access to the records as part of her normal duties as an assistant, if the build was one of their current projects, so she really wouldn't be accessing any information that she wasn't supposed to. If the information happened to help her case, all the better. Kelsey still felt kind of guilty for trying to get dirt on Brad from the C&Y Construction office records, but she vowed she would do her usual excellent work and, hopefully, gather the ammunition she needed without getting Deke and his company into hot water. The ladies toasted to Kelsey and wished her luck before heading to their own homes.

CHAPTER SEVEN

Kelsey spent the weekend watching movies and playing games with Charlie. She wanted to reassure him that she was fine after her accident, so she tried hard to make his weekend fun. By Sunday evening, Charlie had stopped asking her if she was okay or making any reference at all to her accident, so she was confident that he had dealt with what had happened to her and come through unscathed. With Charlie squared away, Kelsey was ready to get started on Operation Snag-a-Man. Monday morning, Kelsey popped up out of bed before the alarm, got Charlie off to the school bus in record time and sat down with a cup of coffee and the telephone. She looked C&Y Construction's number up on the internet and was about to dial when her office telephone rang. The number was local and the caller I.D. read "Connelly, D."

"Hello, Total Office Solutions. This is Kelsey."

"Hi, Kelsey, it's Deke Connelly. Did I catch you at a good time?"

His deep, sexy voice excited all kinds of warm tingles in her lady parts."Yes, actually, I was just about to call you. I wanted to follow-up with you about your company's need for a new website and office assistance. I have some time in my schedule over the next couple of weeks and I would be happy to work with you, if you are ready to get started." Kelsey felt like she was babbling, but she continued on. "I mean, if you still want help. I don't know if you've had a website designer give you a quote before, but I am very reasonable and I'd be happy to offer you a discount since you saved my life and all, and I have references if you need them." Kelsey stopped talking when her lungs burned from lack of oxygen. She took a breath and Deke jumped in.

"Absolutely!" He gave a short laugh. "Can I take you to breakfast and discuss what you think we need?"

"Oh." Kelsey sat there for a second, stunned that she hadn't had to work harder to convince Deke to consider hiring her. "Sure! When are you free?"

"Honey, I'm free every day. The Constitution says so!" Once again, Deke laughed.

Kelsey couldn't keep from smiling. His jokes were so lame, but it was so endearing!

Deke continued, "I'm down at the county courthouse, I just finished pulling some permits. According to the address on your business card, I'm not too far from you. What about meeting right now? It's not raining, so we should be safe."

Kelsey looked down at the sweat pants and ratty college t-shirt she had thrown on after her morning shower. Her "office" was her third bedroom, so she rarely dressed up for her fifteen-foot commute from the living room. She would need to spruce up her typical "business casual" look before she left the house so she wouldn't scare the neighbors. At least her hair had dried. She could whip herself into shape in less than twenty minutes. Her quick change ability was her superpower.

"Give me half an hour and I can meet you. How about the

Sacred Grounds Coffee Shop over on Main?" The locally owned café was a two-block walk from Kelsey's house. She had a soft spot for their blueberry muffins. Deke agreed and they hung up. Kelsey leapt from her office chair and hurried into the bedroom, shedding comfort clothes along the way. She changed, styled her naturally wavy brown hair, and applied a little makeup with ten minutes to spare for the short walk to the coffee shop. The thought of seeing Deke again placed an extra spring in her step.

CHAPTER EIGHT

Deke gave a fist pump while pushing the off button on his phone. He'd taken a chance calling this early, but he couldn't stop himself. He had been thinking about Kelsey non-stop since his visit to the hospital. Even though he tried to put her out of his mind once he knew that she would recover from her injuries, his subconscious wouldn't let him. When he ran into her at the doctor's office, he figured Karma was giving him a big High-Five in the middle of his forehead. Now he'd never stop thinking about her until he'd gotten to know her better. Every set of dimples he saw reminded him of the little dents in Kelsey's cheeks that popped up when she smiled. Every woman in a pair of jeans reminded him of the sweet sway of Kelsey's denim-covered backside the day he first spotted her. Deke's immediate attraction and his libido weren't going to give him peace until he learned whether they were any good together.

His cock had been at least semi-hard since he had first seen her striding across his building lot in the rain. He liked curvy women and he had enjoyed watching the sway of her heart-shaped ass as she picked her way carefully across the muddy lot. She hadn't even glanced around when she pulled up across the street. He knew she didn't know he was there in his truck, which freed him to thoroughly check her out. He had been thinking about what he would like to do to that luscious ass when the lightning struck and she went down.

His stomach had dropped. He'd jumped from his truck and rushed to her side. When she woke up, immense relief swept through him. When she looked at him like she wanted to lick him all over, his cock had hardened despite the fact she was hurt and not in her right mind. After sending her off in the ambulance, Deke had fought his instinct to follow and make sure she was okay. He didn't even know her name, but he felt drawn to her. Since that day, she kept showing up in his dreams. During last night's nocturnal wanderings, she had shown up at the door of his hunting cabin dressed in jeans, but completely drenched, just like when he'd first seen her. Unlike his real life experience, though, Dream Kelsey had looked at him with lust-filled eyes and begged him to help her out of her wet clothes. He had helped her undress, pulling off one damp piece of clothing at a time until she stood before him with all of her luscious curves bared. She raised her hands to push the damp hair out of her face and her breasts lifted, drawing his attention their dark pink nipples. Just as he was about to lift her pillowy breasts to his mouth to taste those hard little buds, the alarm on his phone went off and startled him awake. His cock had been so hard that it ached as he got up to shower.

He had continued to think about the generous curves revealed by her thin hospital gown while he tried to bring the raging erection under control. Did she have dark brown curls on her mound, or did she shave her pubic hair? God, he loved a smooth pussy. He stroked himself to release. He didn't want anything in the way of his tongue as he licked a woman to completion. If she didn't shave or wax, maybe he could convince Kelsey to let him shave her.

He was so distracted by thoughts of lathering and trimming Kelsey's lady biscuit that he nicked his cheek while shaving. She was fast becoming a big distraction. Hopefully, he could get her out of his thoughts and into his bed...soon.

Deke lost his virginity to his Junior Year, High School girlfriend in the back of his dad's Oldsmobile. Since then, he'd come close to settling down a few times, but something had always stopped him from popping the question. He respected women, knew how to satisfy them, and had never lacked for willing bed partners, but made no promises about settling down and raising a family. At 38-years-old, he was too focused on making something of himself. If he ever started a family, he wanted time to focus on his wife instead of his next paycheck. He didn't want his wife or child to struggle like his own family had, especially after his dad's sudden death.

Deke had grown up modestly as the son of farming parents in a close-knit little town in North Central Kentucky. They weren't rich, but they were happy. Near the end of Deke's Senior Year of High School, when his dad died of a heart attack while cutting tobacco in the east field, life changed drastically. Deke's mom had never thought to be anything but a farmer's wife. His parents had never considered the possibility of either of them dying young, so they had never thought to buy any kind of life insurance. The farm still had a mortgage and Deke and his younger brother had tried to make a go of it with the help of a few of their neighbors for another year, but the economy tanked. Tobacco prices dropped to an all-time low and Deke's mom couldn't make up the difference to meet the mortgage payments with her meager waitress' salary. His mom had to sell the farm and move him and his brother in with her parents in order to cover their debts. Deke's grandparents had also been tobacco farmers, but by the time they had moved in, his grandfather had leased his land to a co-op and made just enough to keep food on the table and pay the property taxes. It had about killed him, watching his mom suffer.

He had felt like a failure that had let his dad down when they lost the farm. Deke never wanted his mom to feel loss like that again. He had buckled down in school and picked up any part time job that he could to help earn money to help his mom and grandparents. He knew farming didn't pay well. He kept his grades up working forty to fifty hours a week, breaking his back for a few dollars an hour helping neighbors work their land.

After watching their small town farmers struggle for years, Deke knew that he didn't want to farm. Before he had even graduated, he applied and was accepted to Northern Kentucky University. As soon as he got his diploma , he moved to Highland Heights and rented an apartment by campus. To pay for college, he worked summers pouring concrete and hanging drywall for some local home builders. He had found his niche. He studied business and accounting and worked full-time learning all there was to know about building houses. By the time he graduated, he had worked his way up to foreman and oversaw the building of several popular subdivisions. He met Eli Yates at his first subdivision job and they became friends. Eli was a newly graduated architect who worked on several of the projects Deke oversaw. The two worked well together, and when the family that ran the company sold to a competitor, Deke and Eli made the leap to opening their own company. C&Y Construction was only six years old, but they had developed a great reputation for on-time, on-budget, custom-designed luxury homes and their business was booming. Deke's business was his passion, but his bank account didn't keep his bed warm at night. So when a certain blue-eyed web designer arrived in a flash of lightning, he thought that he might finally be able to add a little sizzle to his spreadsheets.

Deke spotted Kelsey through the window of the little neighborhood coffee shop as he parked his truck across the street. She sat at a table for two with a couple of take out cups and some giant muffins in front of her. When Deke walked in, she raised her hand and gave him a little wave and a smile. God, her smile lit up her face and made her blue eyes shine. Deke knew he had it bad when his heart beat a little faster at the sight of the dimples in her cheeks. Deke took a deep breath to stop his cock from saluting her when he imagined running his hands through all of that thick, luscious hair. Next time he had that hair in his lap, he hoped for something more fun than checking for a head injury.

"Hey there, Honey! You didn't have to get my coffee for me, but I sure appreciate it," Deke said as he joined her at the little table. Kelsey reached out her hand to shake his, in a very businesslike manner, but Deke wasn't having it. He took her hand, pulled her from her seat and into a hug. He pulled her tightly into an embrace, smashing her warm breasts against his chest and rubbing up and down her back a couple of times before releasing her. The little hitch in her breath told him that he had surprised her, but she hadn't pulled out of his arms, either. Deke took that as a good sign that she was feeling the attraction between them, too. Kelsey's cheeks were flushed with a rosy glow that hadn't been there before their embrace, so he hoped that was a sign that she felt the same spark that he felt.

Deke let her go and grabbed the cup of coffee by the empty chair. "I'll add some cream and sugar and be right back." Deke turned toward the coffee fixings bar and felt the heat of Kelsey's stare on his backside as he walked away. He smiled. Hey, he would take whatever attention she wanted to give him. After doctoring up his coffee just the way he liked it, Deke headed back and took a seat across from Kelsey. She was crumbling one of the muffins and wouldn't meet his gaze.

"You look great, Honey. Are you feeling good?" he asked. She finally turned her attention away from the baked good she was torturing and met his gaze tentatively, a smile crinkling her eyes.

"I'm fine, actually. Except for needing a new cell phone, you wouldn't know I'd come that close to kicking the bucket." Kelsey's joke fell a little flat. Deke could tell she was still a little hinky about her brush with death.

"So, let's talk about your website," Kelsey said as she reached for a portfolio in the carry-all by her feet.

"Are you in a hurry? I'd just as soon finish my coffee and help you put that other muffin out of its misery before we get started on the more serious stuff." Deke smiled, and Kelsey saw a twinkle in his bright green eyes. "According to an ancient proverb, now that I've saved your life, I'm responsible for you . I have to make sure you're eating breakfast. It's the most important meal of the day, you know."

Kelsey regarded him skeptically as she dropped the flap back over her messenger bag and reached for a piece of her nearly decimated blueberry muffin. "You sure seem to get a lot of life advice from the ancient Chinese," she said drolly.

"What can I say? I eat a lot of takeout. The Oriental Wok in Fort Mitchell is my favorite. They always throw in a couple of extra fortune cookies. I've taken advice from worse sources." Deke saw Kelsey smile before she popped a hunk of muffin into her mouth. When she began to chew, she closed her eyes and moaned softly. That moan made his little brain perk up and start to stand at attention. He shifted, hoping to find a little more room in his suddenly tight jeans. "I guess you really like blueberry muffins?"

Kelsey opened her eyes and smiled, blushing as she swallowed. "Well, what can I say? I like the muffins here. I have to have one at least once a week and I missed my fix while I hung out at my parents' recovery prison. I think there is crack or something sprinkled all over the top."

"Good to know.... So I dangle a blueberry muffin and you'll do my bidding?" Deke raised his paper cup and took a sip to cover his teasing smile. He swallowed and schooled his features into an innocent guise.

Kelsey narrowed her eyes in mock suspicion. "Do you screen all of your potential business associates based upon whether or not you can bribe them to get your way?"

"Nope! Only the pretty ones." Deke laughed as he popped the last bit of muffin into his mouth and brushed the crumbs from his hands.

"You are a flirt." Kelsey sipped her coffee and fished the last of the blueberry muffin crumbs off her plate.

"Is it working?" Deke asked, waggling his thick black eyebrows.

Kelsey rolled her eyes and laughed. "Now, why would I voluntarily tip my hand by telling you? I think we should get back to business." She again reached for her work portfolio and a pen from the messenger bag at her feet. She had brought several examples of landing pages and website designs she had done for other customers to try to get an idea of what Deke and his partner were looking for. She also withdrew a blank legal pad for jotting down notes and design ideas that struck her during their conversation. It was better to get the customer's buy-in from the very beginning of the design process, rather than surprise them with a completed concept.

"I pulled up your current website earlier to familiarize myself with what you already have, but I would like you to take a look and tell me what you would like to see." Kelsey handed him a copy of the web pages she had printed off after he called. She scooted closer so they could share the copies and she caught a whiff of Deke's citrus aftershave. She took a deep breath, closed her eyes and smiled. She really was going to have to rethink her position on Key Lime pie. She shook her head slightly to clear the less-than-business-like images of a shirtless Deke feeding her tangy bites from his own fork. She turned to ask Deke if he had any first impressions but froze when his head moved toward her. His soft lips pressed her startled ones and she automatically opened her mouth in surprise. Deke must have taken this as a positive reaction because his lips pressed hers a little harder and his tongue slide over her bottom lip as he lifted his hand up into the hair at the back of her head. Her mind went completely blank. His kiss was so unexpected, she had no time to think...only to react. Kelsey kissed him back, tentatively at first, then with a touch of the pent up passion she had been trying to hide from him since she first locked eyes with him in the rain.

Deke's hold on the back of her head was gentle, but Kelsey couldn't have torn her lips from his for anything short of a national emergency. This was the single hottest kiss she had ever experienced...*ever.* Her mind screamed at her to stop, this was supposed to be a business meeting, but her heart was having *none* of that noise. Since the rest of her body seemed to be on board with Team Kiss the Man, there was no convincing her lips to stop moving sensuously over Deke's luscious mouth or to stop her hands from drifting up his torso to massage his chest. Her nipples were getting hard and her panties were getting wet. She started to breathe hard and deepened the kiss by fisting her hands in the material of his shirt and pulling him toward her.

Deke flinched and broke the kiss.

"Careful, there, Honey...my shirt's not all you're pulling." He unwrapped her fingers from his shirt to release the chest hairs that she had yanked but he didn't release her hands.. Instead, he placed her flattened hands onto his chest and covered her hands with his. He then proceeded to rub her hands up and down the injured area. She could feel his nipples harden and understood how turned on he was.

Kelsey's eyes widened as she came back to her senses and realized that, not only had she made out with a potential client in the middle of a café, she had actually hurt said potential client by losing her senses and trying to maul him.

"Oh my god, I am so sorry! I don't know what just happened." Kelsey's face burned while the blood pumped in her ears. She looked frantically around the coffee shop, trying to determine who had seen her grope Deke. She wondered if a person could pass out from embarrassment. She tried to pull her hands back but he wouldn't let go.

"Kelsey, look at me," Deke ordered quietly. Kelsey raised her confused and slightly panicked gaze to lock eyes with Deke.

"I'm not sorry. I've been wanting to do that since I saw you awake and trying so hard to cover yourself with the sheet on your bed at the hospital." He smiled slightly. "Probably, even before that, but even I draw the line at kissing women that have just be struck by lightning, no matter how hot I think they look in their jeans."

Kelsey's eyes widened and her concern about the rest of the patrons in the café faded. She could only seem to focus on the broad, firm chest of the man directly in front of her. "You thought I looked hot in my jeans?"

"Oh yeah. I noticed you right away striding across that muddy lot. You were stomping and your beautiful backside was swinging from side to side. I was practically hypnotized. I'd been sitting in my truck making some notes when you drove up. You were so focused on walking and dialing your phone that I knew you hadn't seen me." Deke continued to hold her hands to his chest so she wouldn't pull away. "I was thinking really hard about all the things I'd like to do to that beautiful ass of yours when the lightning hit. It certainly wasn't the way I wanted to get to know you, though, and I'm really glad that you're okay."

❦

Kelsey looked up at him, unmoving, and he watched her breathing slow as she visibly relaxed. He didn't want to scare her away, but there was no way he could have resisted tasting those lips when she scooted so close to him. He prayed he hadn't spooked her too much with his lack of control. He had only meant it to be a soft introduction to the idea that he thought of her as more than a potential web designer, to see how she reacted. When she had kissed him back, their passion had sparked and neither one of them could do much but deepen the kiss. It was becoming obvious that this woman completely short-circuited his self-control. When he finally got her alone, he knew they were going to be amazing together.

As Kelsey tugged her hands from his grip took a minute straighten the paperwork that had scattered when she leaned across the table to deepen their kiss, a strange look passed over her face. She looked directly up at him with an unflinching gaze and demanded, "Do you really even want a web site re-design or was this just an excuse to try to get into my pants?" Kelsey held his gaze and waited for his answer.

"Honestly, what I see is an opportunity, not an excuse, to spend time with you and convince you to give me a chance to kiss your beautiful lips again, but Eli and I really have been looking to upgrade our web image. As you can tell by our current web page, we're obviously not experts in web design. We know we need an update, but don't know where to start to look for help. When you explained what you did at your company, it seemed like a great fit. If I get to know you better, well that's just a bonus. I'm not just looking for an excuse to get into your pants. I'm pretty sure they won't fit me." Deke gave a short laugh. He could tell she was uncomfortable with the kiss they had just shared. His corny joke seemed to do the trick as he watched the dimples pop in her cheeks.

"You nerd!" Kelsey blurted, as she lifted one of her hands and smacked him gently on the shoulder. She gave a little laugh and turned back to her printouts.

"I prefer the term *Intellectual Badass* rather than nerd, but you can call me anything you want as long as you call me," Deke retorted.

"Oh my god, you've got to stop! I'm going to snort coffee out of my nose! No more cheesy pickup lines," Kelsey laughed. "Let's get back to your website."

"Okay, okay." Deke held up his hands in surrender. He was relieved to have gotten Kelsey to relax. It was clear from her kiss that she was just as interested in him, but her nervousness afterward screamed loud and clear that she was not comfortable rushing into anything physical. He could understand that. She had a kid and he figured that her divorce from that pansy-ass Taggert hadn't been pretty. With any other woman, even a hint of that sort of baggage had caused Deke to back away from any sort of entanglement. He avoided high maintenance women. Kelsey was different in that she didn't seem to want anything from him. She appeared capable of making a good life for herself on her own. Deke admired her drive to succeed. He saw it in the mirror every day when he looked at his own face. Kelsey had a softness to her nature, though, that he lacked. She was all soft curves and flexibility while he was hard angles and unbending. Her softness inexorably awakened his protective instincts *and* his sexual interest. That combo hadn't happened in longer than Deke could remember...if ever.

He and Kelsey sipped coffee refills and planning out C&Y Construction's new internet presence until lunch time. Kelsey clearly knew her way around the virtual world and asked intelligent questions about Eli's and his company and their business plans. Deke also appreciated that Kelsey didn't try to wheedle information about her ex-husband out of him over coffee. He started to raise the subject of Brad's financial situation, but Kelsey looked at her watch.

"I am so sorry! I didn't realize so much time had passed. I have to meet another client via teleconference at 11:00 a.m. I have about twelve minutes to get back." Kelsey began gathering her papers and stuffing them into her messenger bag.

"I can drop you off. Then I'll know where to picture you while I'm thinking about that kiss for the rest of the day." The tight stretch of his jeans across his lap was unlikely to let him forget that kiss. "C'mon, I'm just parked across the street."

Kelsey thanked him and said, "That would be great. It's usually only a ten minute walk, but I don't want to be late."

Deke gathered their dirty dishes, placed them on the counter for the café staff, and led Kelsey out to his truck. He helped her into the passenger seat of his black pick-up, closed her door and made his way around to the driver's side. He got in, started the engine and told her to point him in the right direction as he buckled his seat belt.

Right at the corner, two blocks up, left on Madison and it's the third house on the right. White with black shutters and a red front door. You can't miss it. Thanks a lot for doing this. I really appreciate it."

Deke eased into traffic and followed the simple directions.

"No problem. When do you think you will have a proposal for our website redesign?" Deke asked.

"I'll have it ready in a couple of days. I will email it to you and you can call me when you're ready to discuss it."

Deke was able to pull up right in front of Kelsey's little bungalow. "How about I take you to dinner Friday night and we'll talk about it then?" he asked. He knew she was in a rush, so he gambled and didn't give her time to over-think her response.

Kelsey didn't hesitate. "I'd like that, but I have to make sure I can get a sitter. I'll ask my parents and get back to you." She unbuckled her seat belt and reached for the door handle.

Deke grabbed her arm before she could jump from the truck. He pulled her gently but surely toward him and kissed her. The kiss was brief but intense, meant to show that the kiss in the coffee shop was not a one-time thing. Deke wanted Kelsey to understand that he planned on seeing where this relationship could go. "Unless you call me to cancel, I will be here at 7:00 Friday night to pick you up. We'll go casual." He smiled. "In fact, why don't you wear those jeans again?" Kelsey looked at his grinning face and just shook her head. She jumped from the truck with a smile, turned and waved. "I'll see what I can do. Thanks for the ride."

Deke watched her until she unlocked her door and went in after turning and giving him a small wave and a smile. *Oh yeah*, he thought, *I got the dimples*! The thought of making her smile was enough to make him happy. That was a first. Now he knew he *definitely* had it bad for Kelsey Taggert. Too bad the details he had dug up on her ex-husband weren't likely to help her collect the child support he owed. In fact, according to the few documents he located, the house had been paid for out of some kind of trust. Even though they were divorced and Kelsey didn't get any of the money, surely her kid still got the benefits, right? Isn't that how rich people did things? Kelsey didn't seem like the type of woman to make accusations that she didn't have proof to support, but he didn't understand why she would make such a fuss over a few thousand dollars if her kid was a millionaire. He just hoped this mess with her ex-husband didn't place him on the wrong side of her fight.

CHAPTER NINE

After her meeting with Deke, the rest of Kelsey's week seemed to fly. Her first date in over a decade somehow crept up on her and she felt understandably nervous, knowing she was hopelessly rusty on dating etiquette. While Deke Connelly really revved her motor, something about his personality made her so comfortable. Maybe it was his corny jokes...it was hard to be intimidated by a man that owned his lame jokes as much as Deke did.

She was anxious to see Deke again, but preparing for her first date in over fifteen years was still nerve-wracking. She had enlisted all of her friends' help and advice on getting ready for the big night. Each of the four women had been forced to calm Kelsey down as she freaked out about some little detail or another as the days marched by. To do casual, she didn't need a new outfit, but she wanted to look her best. She booked a half-day at the salon and spa where she usually got her hair cut and decided to purchase the works: hair, manicure, pedicure and waxing. After all, nothing says unsexy like a lady with a beard, right?

So many things surprised her about her body as she aged,

but she would never get used to the weird increase in body hair. Since she was getting waxed in several areas, she made the appointment for Wednesday morning so she would have plenty of recovery time before she had to apply cosmetics. Della opted to join her and they sat in the spa's welcome room, soaking their feet in cucumber water and sipping hot tea as they waited for their first appointments.

"So," Della said, "are you getting waxed *everywhere*?" She waggled her eyebrows. Even though they were the only women in the cozy little waiting room, Della refrained from getting too specific, in case anyone they didn't know walked in.

"Well," Kelsey said, "I'm getting my lip, chin and brows done, for sure, and I am contemplating a bikini wax. I just don't want to jinx anything by making assumptions about how far this thing will go. It's only our first date, after all."

"Who cares? Even if it doesn't work out with Deke, we made a pact to rev up get our sex lives. We'll all get laid eventually, so you might as well start preparing the equipment for the party. You have *got* to get a Brazilian. It hurts like a bitch but you will not believe how sexy you will feel once it's done." Kelsey looked at Della like she HAD to be joking, but Della stared back at her in all seriousness. "Do it! If you want to be sexy, you have to feel sexy. Trust me, it's amazing. I had one done right before the last vacation Dave and I want on and he went *crazy* for it." Della very rarely talked about Dave, so Kelsey knew she meant what she said.

"Okay," Kelsey said. "I'll do it. Besides, if I don't like it, it will just grow back, right? What do I have to lose?"A pretty, brunette spa employee entered and introduced herself as Lydia, the aesthetician that would be doing Kelsey's waxing. Lydia guided Kelsey back to one of the private spa treatment rooms and confirmed that she was getting both facial and bikini waxing during their session. Kelsey almost lost her nerve when the aesthetician instructed her to remove all of her clothing from the waist down and handed her a hand towel to preserve her modesty, then left Kelsey in the waxing room to get undressed.

A hand towel? Seriously? What was she supposed to cover with that? At least the gynecologist gave her an entire sheet, even if it was made of paper thin enough to serve as a dinner napkin.

Kelsey did as instructed and laid on the padded table. Two minutes later, Lydia returned and asked Kelsey if she had any concerns or skin sensitivity issues that she wanted to discuss. Kelsey assured Lydia that waxing usually left her a little red, but she recovered within twenty four hours. Lydia had a calm and efficient manner that put Kelsey at ease. She seemed pleasant enough as she cleansed Kelsey's face and gently patted it dry. As she applied warm wax to Kelsey's face and quickly removed it with thin strips of fabric, she made small talk. As she shaped Kelsey's brows, they discussed their children. As she denuded Kelsey's lip of the thin layer of dark hair that had sprouted after her thirty-eighth birthday, they discussed the area's recent drought. As she tugged the unwanted fur from Kelsey's chin, they chatted about the price of gasoline. It was all perfectly tolerable, if not pleasant, until Lydia began the bikini wax.

"I see from your ticket that you are interested in a Brazilian wax. Do you want the full Brazilian, or the partial Brazilian?"

"Uh, this is my first venture to South America, so to speak. What is the difference?" Kelsey asked.

"A full Brazilian removes all the hair from your genital and anal region. A partial Brazilian leaves some hair at the top of your pubic area. If you go with the partial, you can have the remaining hair shaped."

"Shaped?" Kelsey asked. "Into what?"

“Well, the ’landing strip’ is the most popular, but I have done diamonds, hearts, arrows and initials, but that much detail is extra, since it requires clippers,” Lydia explained in a very matter-of-fact tone.

“All of that is just too much work,” Kelsey replied. “I am going for the full Brazilian.”

“Ready to start?" Lydia asked.

Kelsey nodded once to confirm and Lydia continued her explanation of the steps. "Since the hair is more coarse in this area, I will actually be using a cold wax,” Lydia explained as she rolled her cart toward Kelsey’s hip. Lydia continued to prepare her station as she explained after-care, including over-the-counter pain medication to ease the discomfort and inflammation, as well as soothing creams that the spa offered for sale at the front. Lydia whipped off Kelsey’s little hand towel and asked her to spread her legs slightly.

Kelsey tried hard not to be embarrassed, but she was not used to anyone starting at her lady garden, much less assessing the area for improvements. While Lydia wore gloves and maintained a very professional demeanor, no amount of small talk could make Kelsey relax while a virtual stranger stared at her most intimate area. Kelsey tried to chat with Lydia, like she had done during the facial waxing, about upcoming vacations and recent movies, but the other woman seemed to be taking an inordinately long time to get started. Kelsey started wondering, *What is she looking at? Am I super hairy or something? Is she making mental notes so that she can write some kind of article for a professional journal on freakishly hairy women? Is there some kind of weird mole down there?* Finally, the aesthetician spread on the first stick full of wax. Kelsey took a deep breath, and Lydia painted the first area with a purple, slightly warm depilatory. Lydia positioned one gloved hand on the inside of Kelsey's thigh to pull the skin taut. Kelsey stared at the ceiling and asked, “Is there any place around here that you would recommend for lun— SWEET MOTHER OF GOD!" Kelsey yelled. Lydia used the hand not holding Kelsey's quivering thigh to tear a strip of hair from her poor, abused crease with what was *clearly* sandpaper covered in battery acid. The pain was so intense that Kelsey couldn't take in a breath.

"The first one is always the hardest," Lydia calmly declared as she applied more torture paste to Kelsey's abused pubic region. As Lydia removed the second strip of cold hair remover, Kelsey had to disagree. The second strip *definitely* hurt as much as the first one. "Son of a motherless goat!" she belted out, as the third strip of her dignity was removed. What in the hell had she ever done to Della for her to wish this kind of pain on someone she claimed to be her best friend? "Fuck a duck!" Kelsey gave up any attempt to control the expletives flowing from her mouth like hot lava and concentrated on breathing though the pain.

Little Ms. Lydia continued to coolly rip hair out of the most sensitive area of Kelsey's body without flinching at the cussing.

Clearly, her mother, who had tried to convince her that there was never a time when cursing made anything better, had never had hot lava poured on her pink parts and then ripped off. Oh my god, the pain! She tried to remember the deep breathing exercises the Lamaze coach had taught her when she was preparing to deliver Charlie, but then she remembered that all of that bullshit hadn't helped a damn bit with the pain.

"Pull your left leg up to your chest," Lydia ordered.

Kelsey complied, more out of fear than willing cooperation.

"Press your leg out, like a chicken wing," demanded the petite drill sergeant. As the commands to bend her lower extremities into bizarre, uncomfortable positions continued like a masochist's game of hokey pokey, Kelsey became even more convinced that Della was, in fact, avenging some horrible sin that Kelsey had unknowingly committed. There was *no way* this could *ever* be worth it. She couldn't stop now, though. A person did not get just half of her love triangle waxed. She would look ridiculous.

"Now roll over on your knees and pull your butt cheeks apart," the aesthetician ordered. Kelsey hesitated and Lydia explained, "I've got to clean up the rest of the area and I can't access it any other way. The good news is, it's almost over," she chirped. That's the good news, Kelsey wondered? Then what's the bad news?

Apparently, the bad news was that "cleaning up the rest of the area" was Wax Bitch speak for ripping the hair off her asshole! Sweet Jeezus on a three-humped camel! If Kelsey thought that the front was painful, she had run out of words to describe the sheer burning hell of having hair ripped from her anus. She was in such pain and so exhausted that she just kneeled there and whimpered. Lydia finished up by applying a soothing cream to Kelsey's abused skin, which at least stopped the constant burning sensation.

She couldn't move. She didn't even have the wherewithal to lay down after Lydia informed her that she was finished. Kelsey just crouched there like a feral cat, waiting to be attacked, but too exhausted to fight back.

"I'll give you a few minutes to get dressed," Lydia murmured in a low voice as she cleaned up her station and tidied up the room. " I've left a sheet here on the counter detailing the aftercare instructions we talked about earlier. Take your time getting dressed and have a nice day." Lydia quietly exited the room.

"Have a nice day," Kelsey mumbled. "I'll show you a *nice day*. Bitch. You just say shit like that because you know I can't catch you right now. Have a nice day, my ass."

Kelsey kept up her litany of wishing evil on both Lydia and her good friend Della while she somehow managed to pull on her panties and shorts. When she opened the door, she found Della lingering in the hall. The other woman didn't say a word, but held out her hands. One hand cradled two pain relievers and the other held a bottle of water. Kelsey snatched both, downed the pills, guzzled the water and gave Della a death glare. Della smirked.

"I hate you," Kelsey declared.

"Oh, I know you do right now," Della confirmed, "but you will *love* me the first time Deke sees your shiny Little Miss Muffet and starts eating all of your curds and whey...with his tongue."

Kelsey pointed her index finger at her former friend. "It had better be worth it, or I'm going to make an appointment for you and stand outside the door while she does the exact same thing to you!" Kelsey turned to find the spa concierge waiting to direct them to their nail appointments. She refused to speak to Della for the rest of their time at the spa. She sent her dirty looks and sipped cucumber water, wondering if the literal pain in her ass was ever going to cease. After manis and pedis, they were whisked away to different hair stations and Kelsey didn't see Della again until she returned to the lobby, ready to check out.

Della let out a low wolf whistle and made a motion with her hand for Kelsey to turn around and show off from all angles. "You look absolutely gorgeous, Honey! Loki isn't going to know what hit him."

"I am still mad at you, but you're right. I look fabulous!" Kelsey tried to keep an aggrieved look on her face to make Della pay for the horrible bikini waxing advice, but she felt too good about herself not to smile. "You, however, are still a Bitch. I am not sure if I will ever forgive you...or that I am ever going to be able to evacuate my bowels again in this lifetime. There is NO WAY that my ass is ever going to unclench again. In fact, I think someone wrote a song about a 'Burning Ring of Fire' just for me," Kelsey said with all seriousness.

"You can curse me all you want right now, but you will thank me later!" Della said in a singsong voice as they walked out of the salon. They were both plucked, trimmed, highlighted, low-lighted and polished within an inch of their lives and, Kelsey had to admit, she hadn't looked this good in years....if ever. She turned to Della as they made their way to their separate cars and said, "I'll let you know when you are forgiven."

Della gave a little laugh. "I'll bet you a dozen Blueberry Muffins from Sacred Grounds that you are sitting at your kitchen table writing me a thank you note for the happy treatment *your* muffin gets on date night."

Kelsey shouted, "You're on!" as she delicately slid behind the wheel and headed back to the office.

CHAPTER TEN

Kelsey spent the next week up to her elbows in client work, and she was more than ready to cut loose and relax by the time Friday rolled around. She was putting the finishing touches on her hair when knuckles rapped against her front door. She glanced at the clock. Five minutes before seven. She was more than ready to spend some real-life time with Deke. He'd spent so much time walking across her thoughts this week that she swore he'd worn a path through her brain. She was more excited for this date than she had been for any date that she could remember. Her libido cheered and did a little dance in her panties every time Deke came to mind.

Hopefully, they could get the business part of their evening over with quickly so she could feel him out about Operation Get Kelsey Some Orgasms. If that kiss the other day was anything to go by, Deke was definitely interested in her physically, so getting him to put out shouldn't be too much of a challenge. What red-blooded man turned down no-strings-attached sex? Kelsey was pretty sure that her dry streak was over and that if Deke made love anywhere near as well as he kissed, then she would be one happy camper.

Charlie had been invited to a sleepover with a school buddy, so Kelsey hadn't had to scramble for a baby sitter. Maybe all the planets were aligning so that she could have a good time for once. She wore her favorite cherry red, v-neck cashmere sweater and the same jeans she had worn on the day of her accident, as requested. Her wavy hair softly brushed her shoulders and she had kept her makeup to a minimum. After all, she didn't want too much makeup rubbing off all over Deke's face when she plastered her lips against his.

Grinning, Kelsey practically bounced toward the front door and yanked it open. The smile faded when she saw her ex-husband Brad standing in the doorway instead of her hot contractor man.

"Brad?" Kelsey asked, exasperated. "What are you doing here?

"I'm here to pick Charles up. Tell him to hurry it up. We're late for our reservations at the club. I actually thought he would be on the porch waiting for me, like I told you in my message. Didn't you get my text?" Brad's condescending tone made Kelsey's blood boil. He wasn't even looking at her. He was just pecking out a message on his smart phone and shifting weight from foot to foot.

"Your text?" Kelsey asked, exasperated. "No, I didn't get your text, but even if I did, you couldn't take Charlie tonight. He was invited to a sleepover. This is not your weekend. You were scheduled *last* weekend, remember? You are every *other* weekend. Next time, I suggest that you actually *call* instead of assuming that we will rearrange our lives for your last-minute bouts of conscience. Now, if you will excuse me, I have plans." Brad put his hands on his hips and his face took on a petulant guise, like a child told that he can't have a cookie. Kelsey was about to slam the door in Brad's face when Deke's truck pulled up behind Brad's black, late model Mercedes sedan with the dealer plates.

Just GREAT, she thought. There's nothing like your douche nozzle ex-husband meeting your potential new lover at the front door to make for a fun-filled date night. Kelsey took a few steps onto her porch, closing the door behind her. Brad moved back from where he had been crowding the doorway, and Kelsey just looked back and forth between him and the man parking a big black truck in her driveway.

Brad turned to see what Kelsey was looking at and she watched the recognition dawn on Brad's face. "Connelly? What's he doing here?" Brad turned back to Kelsey.

She watched Deke got out of his truck and began to walk up the uneven red brick path to the front porch. He couldn't miss Brad, but he had yet to acknowledge him. Deke looked only at her, and a small smile never left his face. When he reached the stoop, he turned to Brad, said, "Taggert," and offered a nod of acknowledgement before he turned back to Kelsey. Deke smiled broadly as he pulled her into his arms for a brief kiss on her lips and big hug and said, "Hi, Honey. You look good enough to eat! You ready?"

Kelsey turned her face into Deke's chest and inhaled his unique scent of citrus, fresh cured lumber and warm man. She wanted to stay there in his arms for the foreseeable future, especially if Brad would just do her a favor and go away without saying anything else. No such luck.

"Connelly, what are you doing here and how do you know my wife?" Brad demanded in a petulant tone. Kelsey sighed deeply and lifted her head from Deke's chest to look at Brad, who stood on her front porch, staring at both of them with a slightly horrified expression.

"First, *Bradley*, I am your EX-wife. Second, it is none of your business who I spend my time with. That's one of the best parts about being your *ex*-wife," Kelsey answered. "Now, run along. Like I said, I have plans." Kelsey looked up at Deke, who's light green gaze held a distinct twinkle of mischief. "Do you want to come in for a second?"

Brad demanded, "What the hell is going on here? Kelsey, are you screwing my contractor? Oh my god, is this some kind of attempt to ruin my new life with Barbara by causing problems with our house? Now it all makes sense!" Brad pointed a finger at Kelsey and sputtered as he ranted, "I wondered why every little change we requested turned into such a big deal! Now I see that it's some kind of payback! God, you never acted this jealous when we were married." Brad turned to Deke, making slashing motions with his hands. "Is this what you call customer service? Is this the reason why we have had so many up-charges and petty delays? You're fucking my ex and she has convinced you to fuck with me in return? Unbelievable!"

Deke gently, but firmly, shifted Kelsey behind him as he turned to face a red-faced Brad. "Taggert, you had better *never* speak to Kelsey in that tone of voice around me again, or I am going to make sure that you sing Soprano for the rest of your life! Understand?" Deke's tone had deepened with anger, but he never raised his voice. He kept one hand wrapped comfortingly around Kelsey's wrist and rubbed his thumb soothingly over her racing pulse. "You are *way* off base. I met Kelsey when she was injured at our job site. Our personal relationship has nothing to do with you *or* your new home. Now, if you don't want to have to learn how to speak through a swollen mouth and some busted teeth, I suggest that you apologize to the lady."

Both Brad and Kelsey looked at Deke with their mouths gaping. Kelsey's heart was beating out of her chest—not because of what Brad had accused her of, but because Deke had actually stood up for her. No one but her father had *ever* stood up for her before. If she hadn't wanted to climb

Deke Connelly like a tree before, she certainly did right now!

"Are you threatening me?" Brad asked incredulously. "You have *got* to be kidding me. *You* work for ME! I am not apologizing to anyone! If you *dare* to put your hands on me, I will sue you so fast your head will spin!" Brad sputtered the last few words, he was so angry. Funny enough, though, he backed toward his car as he continued to posture and sputter threats. "Threaten me? I don't think so! You'll be hearing from my lawyers. I don't have to put up with this..." Brad's voice faded away as he slid into his car and slammed the door. He barely missed backing into the bumper of Deke's truck as he reversed to clear the car ahead of him. His tires squealed as he pulled into traffic and tore off down the street.

Deke turned to Kelsey and pulled her into his arms. He lowered his mouth to hers briefly and then asked, "You okay, Honey?"

Kelsey sighed and met Deke's concerned gaze. Her eyes welled with tears of frustration and embarrassment. She kept them from falling by looking up at the porch ceiling, but she couldn't control the little hitch in her voice. "I'm fine. Thank you. I am so sorry about that. I didn't know he was going to be here and I opened the door without looking because I thought it was you, but it wasn't and I was trying to get rid of him before you got here, but then you pulled up...." Kelsey knew she was babbling, but couldn't seem to stem the flow of words. Deke put his index finger up to her lips.

"Stop. You do not have to explain anything to me. I'm sorry that I didn't show up a little earlier, like I had wanted to, to stop that crap from happening in the first place." Deke looked at her with a serious expression and asked, "Does he talk to you like that all the time?"

Kelsey gave a short laugh, "No, actually. He rarely says anything to me at all, much less any kind of personal attack.

Brad is so self-absorbed, he rarely acknowledges anyone else's existence. If it isn't about him, he doesn't want to discuss it. That little scene was totally out of character. Of course, he was ticked off because he didn't get his way, so I guess I shouldn't be surprised he threw a tantrum. That's what babies do." Kelsey rolled her eyes and resolved to change the subject. She reached for Deke's chest and made to push out of his embrace, but his embrace tightened. "Enough about him! Let's get back to us...uh, I mean our appointment...you know, about your website."

Deke gave a soft chuckle. "You can call it a date, Kelsey. That's what I meant it to be when I asked. I hope you don't think that I kiss all of my business associates like that." He rubbed small circles on her back and Kelsey became distracted and keyed up. "Mmmmm, this sweater is soft. I could rub on this all night," Deke said in a voice so low that Kelsey thought he might actually be talking to himself. Kelsey turned to open her front door and Deke followed her inside, closing it behind him.

"Well, I didn't want to assume.... I mean, I *wanted* it to be a date, but you said we were going to talk about your webpage...oomph!" Kelsey's sentence cut off as Deke's lips pressing firmly against hers. When he ran his tongue along her lower lip, she opened her lips for his invasion and moaned into his mouth. He raised his hands to frame her face and gently brushed her hair behind her ears. As he broke the kiss he pressed his forehead to hers and asked, "Has anyone ever told you that you talk too much when you're upset?"

"Hmmm?" Kelsey asked, slightly dazed from the kiss. "Well, if you were trying to get me to stop, that was no way to incentivize me," she whispered.

Deke barked a laugh. "Who said I was trying to stop you? It just gives me a chance to help out." Deke pressed little kisses on her forehead, moving along her hairline and down toward her ear. Deke whispered in a gravelly voice, "I love this sweater, honey. It's going to look fantastic on this hardwood floor." He chuckled a little and resumed his assault on her senses. As he got to the shell of her ear, her knees got weak. Deke had discovered a previously unexplored erogenous zone and Kelsey's lady parts awoke and took notice.

"Do you kiss your mother with that mouth?" Kelsey laughed softly. She looked into Deke's laughing eyes and said, "We are supposed to be talking about work," Deke lowered his head like he was going in for a kiss, but Kelsey laughed as she turned her head to avoid his marauding mouth and pushed away from him slightly. "Now, do you want to see the design mockups or do you want to get dinner first?" Her voice was breathy and she unconsciously rubbed her hands up and down Deke's chest.

"Well, that depends," Deke answered. "Are the mockups on a laptop that we can take with us, or do we need to look at them on your equipment here?" He was rubbing circles on Kelsey's lower back that were, slowly but surely, making their way down to her ass. It was mesmerizing and distracting. All the blood in Kelsey's body seemed to be following the unspoken call of Deke's magic hands and concentrating lower body, leaving almost nothing for her brain. It took her a minute to process Deke's question. While she tried to remember what a computer was and why she should care about it, Deke pressed his leg between her thighs and Kelsey unconsciously started rubbing herself on it. The friction was doing delicious things to her pink parts, but was not getting *anything* accomplished on the business front. When she didn't answer after a few seconds, Deke give a small laugh and prompted, "Kels...? Can we look at the stuff on the go?"

"Oh, right!" Kelsey shook her head slightly to clear her thoughts. She pushed against his chest, trying to put a little distance between her throbbing nether regions and Deke's temptingly hard thigh. "Web designs. We can definitely take them with us. I have them on a thumb drive. It will take only a minute....to download... What are you doing to me?"

"Hmmm?" Deke continued to breathe and place small kisses on her ear. When he rimmed the outer shell of her ear with his tongue, she nearly collapsed onto the leg he had wedged between her thighs. He caught her as she slid and held her closer. His hands slid down her back and cupped the cheeks of her ass as he lifted her to make it easier for him to find her mouth with his lips. Deke chased any thoughts but the taste of his kiss right out of her mind as he slid his tongue into her mouth and sensually teased her tongue.

Deke pivoted until he pressed her against the entryway wall, then slid his hands down the back of her thighs and lifted her legs until they wrapped his waist. Kelsey reached around his neck and sank her hands into his thick raven hair. She moaned as his arousal pressed the juncture of her thighs.

Deke pressed closer and began to rub his impressive erection against the seam of her jeans. He cupped her backside and every time his gripped her cheeks he rubbed her clit *exactly* the right way over the bulge in his jeans. Kelsey began to pant as the tiny electrical pulses in her clit came stronger and closer together. When her orgasm hit, she pulled her lips from Deke's questing mouth with a gasp. As her release rolled over her, she squeezed her eyes shut and began to shake in his arms.

She took several deep breaths as her orgasm pulsed and waned, opening her eyes only to look directly into an electric green gaze that was so full of lust she couldn't look away. Kelsey forgot to breathe as she stared, stunned, into Deke's burning gaze.

"You are so fucking beautiful." Deke ground out. He pressed his mouth back onto hers and kissed her so passionately she thought she might just come again. Her nipples were aching points rubbing against his chest with every breath she took, and her pussy still contracted spasmodically, grasping at nothing from the orgasm that she'd just had without this man removing a single article of her clothing. She felt like she could shake out of her own skin...like she had been struck by lightning again. Unlike the last time, this was a wave of pleasure instead of a wave of pain.

Deke broke the kiss and leaned his forehead against hers.

"Oh my god," Kelsey whispered. "I have never had that happen before...you know, with a man...uh, I mean with my clothes on.... I mean— Oh, I don't know what I mean!"

Deke slid her slowly down his body away slightly onto her feet, then backed away slightly. Kelsey sagged against the wall. Kelsey raised her hands to her burning cheeks and looked at the ceiling, then at the floor—anywhere but at Deke. He reached for her hands and held them in his.

"Kelsey, look at me." Deke waited for her to make eye contact. "I'm not going to say I'm sorry. You coming apart in my arms was one of the sexiest things that I have *ever* seen, but that is *not* why I asked you to have dinner with me tonight." He was breathing hard and gently squeezing Kelsey's hands. . "I would love nothing more than to make love to you right now. If you don't want me to carry you to the first soft surface I find in your house and strip you naked, we had better get going," he said in a strangled voice.

It took Kelsey a moment to process that particular thought. The scene that Deke described was exactly what her body wanted him to do. In fact, it was exactly what she and her friends had joked would happen, but something felt off. Her body was willing, but the leftover insecurities from her failed marriage kept popping up in her head like whack-a-mole characters, screaming that it was too soon and that she didn't really know Deke at all. Despite her lower body cheering for horizontal naked time, her head convinced her mouth to make a different call. She knew, without a doubt, that she could never make love to this man and then walk away. He was going to be much too much of a temptation to walk away from. He was a beautiful man, inside and out, but she knew she wasn't ready to put her heart into the game yet. Deke deserved better than to be used to scratch an itch and then tossed aside. She had to slow things down before she lost all control.

So much for having her first unemotional fling!

She slowly pushed away from the wall "It will just take me a minute to get my laptop and the flash drive. I'll be right back." She headed toward her home office. Her mind had won, but only by a slight margin, since her shaky legs had still not recovered from the mind-blowing orgasm she had just enjoyed.

CHAPTER ELEVEN

As Kelsey walked slowly away, Deke tried to calm his racing libido. He silently berated himself for pushing her so far, so fast. He had only meant to distract her from the scene on the front step with her ex-husband. Even in his most vivid fantasies, he had never imagined that she would burn so brightly for him. She was magnificent in her climax. Obviously, her ex-husband was a complete ass. No woman had ever affected Deke like Kelsey Taggert had. Maybe it was some kind of Hero Hangover on his part, but he could see himself with Kelsey in every future scenario that passed through his mind...and he hadn't even seen her naked.

He'd never be able to walk away from a woman as loving and passionate as Kelsey. He didn't want to drive her away before they could see how good they could be together. All of his instincts hold him she was "the one" for him, but she had been hurt by her ex-husband's betrayal. She was skittish. He had to slow down and engage her mind as well as her libido. He suspected that Kelsey had no experience with one night stands. He could tell without asking her. She was smart, beautiful, had a good sense of humor and, most importantly, she had a kid. You didn't mess with a woman like that if you were a decent guy.

He was trying *really* hard to be the patient suitor that she needed instead of a raging bag of lust. He inhaled deeply and blew out a long breath. He would take her to dinner and look at her mockups without jumping her bones. He grimaced. If the blood permanently pooling in his little head instead of his big head was any indication, restraining himself from getting into her panties just *might* kill him.

It only took Kelsey about five minutes to gather what she needed and return to the foyer with her keys, a messenger bag, her purse over her shoulder, and a determined look on her face. She flashed a small smile. She had applied some kind of lip gloss, and her hair looked smoother than it had a few minutes ago. "So, where are we off to?" she asked.

Deke reached for her work bag, slipped its strap over his shoulder, then opened the front door and gestured for her to precede him. "It's a surprise. I have a top secret, taste bud pleasing plan. All you have to do is sit back, relax and enjoy the ride." Kelsey locked the door and they walked to his truck. He opened her door, stowed her messenger bag behind her seat and waited for her to climb up into the truck and get comfortable. He closed her door, walked around the front of the vehicle and climbed into the driver's seat. He started the truck and turned the radio on. "Any preference for radio stations?" he asked.

Kelsey buckled her seatbelt and looked over at him. A mischievous gleam sparkled in her eye and one dimple appeared. "I'm not picky, but just no AC/DC, okay? I've heard enough of 'Thunderstruck' to last me a while," she said. They shared a short laugh as he popped a cd into the dashboard stereo system. The smooth sounds of The Zac Brown Band serenaded them as Deke drove out of Lucky, onto the expressway and headed south.

The sun was starting to set and the sky was burning with deep reds and oranges. They chatted amicably about their favorite restaurants and bands they had seen in concert. Kelsey told Deke some funny stories about sneaking backstage at a summer festival to meet the bands with The Girls, and he told her tales of trouble he had gotten into as a little boy. Kelsey relaxed into the seat and watched Deke's hands on the steering wheel, imagining what they could do to her body. She was seriously enamored of the man and it was making her a little crazy.

She couldn't stop imagining them in intimate situations, even as they discussed which grocery store they thought had the best meat. Deke said he liked a local chain, but Kelsey kept thinking that she would prefer *his* meat, hands down. She was almost appalled at herself....almost. She had never sexualized a man so much in her entire life! She was the mother of a little boy, for god's sake! She would be appalled if some woman thought of Charlie as nothing more than a sex toy...right? So shouldn't she be more respectful of Deke as a human being? Her hormones didn't care whether Deke was an excellent cook or a successful business owner or a humanitarian who saved kittens from burning buildings in his spare time. Those horny bitches just wanted to trace Deke's eight-pack abs with her tongue and then follow his happy trail to paradise. She seriously needed to get a grip.

Deke pulled into the parking lot of a little restaurant simply called "Mary's Place." He switched off the ignition and turned to Kelsey. "I know it doesn't look like much, but you're gonna love it." he said.

"Oh, I love finding new secret places to eat. I'm looking forward to it." Kelsey smiled. They got out of the truck and headed to the front door. When Deke opened the front door, the smell of grilled meat and baked goods hit Kelsey's nose and made her stomach rumble. "Wow, it smells great! My mouth is watering," Kelsey said as she stopped beside the small hostess stand. She glanced around the dining room and spotted a short, middle-aged lady barreling toward them. Her bright red apron read 'Mary's Place.' The woman reached Deke and wrapped her arms around his waist, unable to reach higher. "Deke, Honey! You didn't tell me you were coming!"

"I wanted to surprise you," Deke answered.

The woman released Deke, stepped back and looked up at him. "At my age, I can't do with too many surprises! I'm just glad this is the good kind," she chuckled. She turned a familiar, bright green gaze on Kelsey. "Now who is this pretty lady?"

Deke kept one hand on the woman's shoulder and placed the other on Kelsey's lower back. "This is Kelsey Taggert, the woman I told you about," Deke said. "Kelsey, this is my mom, Phyllis Connelly Stearns."

Kelsey extended her hand, but Phyllis wrapped Kelsey in a warm hug. "Is this the girl that was struck by lightning? Honey, you are a miracle! I have never met anyone who has been struck by lightning before! I'm so glad my boy was there to help you. It's like somebody upstairs is looking out for you. You should definitely play the Power Ball!" Phyllis released Kelsey and looked back and forth between her and Deke.

Kelsey laughed. "That's what everyone tells me. It's very nice to meet you."

"Momma, what's tonight's special?"

"Pork tenderloin with apple and onion compote, your choice of baked or mashed potato, vegetables and dessert. Tucker made pineapple upside down cake yesterday and I know he has a piece or two in the back. Fresh apple pies are tonight's feature." Phyllis rattled off all of this as she wove through the little dining room toward a window table. Of the eight tables in the restaurant, six were full of people who either waved at Deke or called out a greeting. "I know what you want, Deke, but what can I get you to drink, Honey?" Phyllis asked Kelsey.

"Iced Tea, please," Kelsey said.

"Sweet or unsweet?"

"Sweet, please,"

Phyllis smiled. "I knew you were a keeper, Honey. No fake sugar for you!" Phyllis handed them menus and said she would be right back with their drinks and some biscuits.

Kelsey opened her menu and held it up, covering most of her face. She peeked over the top to see Deke staring at her with a twinkle in his eyes. "You passed the iced tea test! Impressive." He grinned.

"You heard your mom. I'm a keeper! You, on the other hand, I'm not too sure about," Kelsey said, and raised an eyebrow.

Deke feigned innocence. "Me? What did I do?"

"Oh, I don't know.... *Maybe* you brought me to meet your mother without even bothering to tell me who she was before we walked in the door."

"I met your mom without warning," Deke said. "Okay, you win. I wanted my mom to meet you. Eli and I eat dinner here a couple times a week and he told her about your accident, so she has been dying to meet you." He looked a little sheepish and his cheekbones acquired a distinctly pink flush. "She is really persistent and I knew she would keep on and on until I caved. Besides, I think I owe you some *pie.*" He jiggled his eyebrows. He knew *exactly* what "pie" would remind her of.

Kelsey tried to keep her face stern, but her resolve buckled under the weight of her mirth upon seeing this big, hulking man turn pink with embarrassment because he wanted someone to meet his mommy. She started giggling and then broke out in a full belly laugh. "You are adorable! You just wanted to show your mommy what you found!"

Kelsey kept laughing. "It's just as adorable as Charlie bringing me that frog he was so proud of catching last week."

"Well, at least I got your dimples to make an appearance. It was totally worth outing myself as a Momma's Boy for that," Deke retorted with a smoldering look in his eyes.

Kelsey blushed.

Her laughter was winding down, but the smile remained her face when Phyllis arrived with their drinks and hot buttermilk biscuits. They gave her their order and made small talk until their meal arrived. Deke was such a pleasant change from her ex. He asked her about her other clients and about how Charlie's day had been. He listened to her answers with interest and told funny stories about his week. Time just flew when they were together...like they had known each other for years, not weeks. They both had the special, which melted in Kelsey's mouth. She forgot to leave room for dessert, so she asked for coffee while Deke polished off the secret stash of pineapple upside down cake *and* her slice of apple pie.

When their meal was finished and the dining room was almost empty, Kelsey looked at Deke and asked, "Ready to get down to business?" Deke nodded, wiping the last remnants of pie from around his mouth. Kelsey pulled her laptop out of her carryall and powered it up. Phyllis meandered around the room cleaning up after the last of the diners and resetting the tables for the next day. Kelsey pushed the computer to the center of the table and turned it so they could both see the screen. She opened the first of her three proposed mockups and began to demonstrate the finer points when Phyllis wandered over and pulled up a chair. Deke and Phyllis listened as Kelsey describe the ideas behind each design and the features she had included, as well as the amount of time needed to maintain each design over time. When she finished, she asked, "Do any of the pages strike your fancy?"

Deke looked at Kelsey with a thoughtful expression. "I actually like all three, but the second one really showcased our designs more than the others and I really liked that. It's what sets us apart from other builders. I also like the one that featured customer testimonials, though. It seems like that would help sell folks who might be on the fence. " Deke looked at Phyllis. "Momma, what do you think?"

Phyllis clapped her hands together and said, "Why can't you have both?"

Kelsey raised her eyebrows and answered, "You absolutely can! I can add any of the features you like from the three mockups to your final web design."

Phyllis smiled and said, "Well, that was easy! Glad I could help." They laughed as the older woman got up. "Kids, I have to close up. You are welcome to sit here as long as you want, but I have to get Tucker home. We have to let the dogs out. Kelsey, it was lovely to meet you!" Phyllis bent over and gave Kelsey a short hug and a kiss on the cheek, then turned and gave Deke the same treatment. "Come back soon."

Kelsey and Deke watched the woman bustle into the foyer, lock the front door, turn the sign in the window to closed and turn out the front lights. Just as she was putting on her jacket and picking up her purse , a short, middle-aged man dressed in black and white chef pants and a white chef's jacket came out of the kitchen. He helped Phyllis with her coat and then they approached Deke and Kelsey's table. Phyllis put her hand on the older man's arm and said, "Tucker, this is the little gal that Deke's been talking about, Kelsey Taggert. Kelsey, this is my husband, Tucker Stearn."

Tucker shook hands with Kelsey then gave Deke the same firm handshake. "Hello, kids! It's good to see you Deke. Kelsey, it's sure nice to put a face to the name. Glad you are okay. You've been the talk of the family ever since Deke told us what happened. You sure are a lucky little lady! You should definitely get some lottery tickets."

They laughed.

"Tucker, the dinner was delicious. It's lovely to meet you," Kelsey said with a genuine smile.

"Well," Phyllis declared, "it's been a long day and it's time for us old folks to head home and put our feet up. You all stay as long as you want." The older couple gave a small wave as they turned, then headed through the dining room toward the swinging doors to the kitchen. "Deke, turn off the coffee pot when you leave and go out the back door. It locks itself. Goodnight, y'all."

Kelsey called out, "Goodnight, Phyllis! Goodnight, Tucker!" at the same time that Deke yelled, "Bye, Momma! 'Night, Tucker!"

As soon as Phyllis and Tucker left through the swinging door, Deke said, "My mom met Tucker at a VFW dance about five years ago. They were widowed young and both had raised their kids alone. Tucker and his wife Mary opened this restaurant about twenty years ago, but she died of cervical cancer five years after it opened. Their daughter April was only three. Tucker and my mom married not long after they met, and she's been working here ever since. Tucker offered to change the name, but my mom wouldn't hear of it. She didn't want to hurt April's feelings, and it didn't bother her that Tucker had loved someone before her. Tucker is a really good guy. I'm happy my mom isn't alone anymore, even though I got an annoying little sister in the bargain." Deke finished with a little laugh.

"Your mom seems like a wonderful lady." Kelsey smiled.

"That she is," Deke replied.

Kelsey appreciated a man who loved his mother. She hoped Charlie felt the same way about her as he grew up. . She didn't want to become the reason that Charlie lost his dad. Brad was a mediocre father, at best, but he was better than no father. She truly hoped she wasn't forced to expose Brad as some sort of criminal at the conclusion of her investigation. If Brad went to jail, she didn't know if Charlie could forgive her for taking his dad away. There was no point in worrying about something that might never happen.

she shook her head While Deke finished the last drop of his sweet tea and another piece of apple pie that he pilfered from the kitchen, they talked about everything under the sun. Deke was funny and a good listener. Kelsey found herself telling him things about herself that she would normally only confide to The Girls. She confessed that she had a few clients that she secretly dreaded hearing from and was trying to work on a way to dump them. She told him all about her college exploits with The Girls and Deke regaled her with stories of the crazy things that he and Eli had dealt with since opening their company. At some point, they both realized it was after ten o'clock. Kelsey asked, "Do you want any more coffee?"

"Nope, I'm good. I think it's too late to hit a movie or anything, but I hate to end our time together. Are you up for a little drive before I take you home?"

Kelsey rolled her eyes to the ceiling and tapped her forefinger against her chin. "Hmmm....I guess...as long as you're not going to drop in on any more of your relatives. I draw the line at one iced tea test per date," Kelsey said.

Deke raised his fist with two fingers raised in the Boy Scout Pledge. "No more relatives...Scout's Honor."

CHAPTER TWELVE

Deke and Kelsey took their dishes to the kitchen, turned off the coffee pot and left the diner. Deke drove to the Devou Park Overlook and parked under a towering oak tree. Across the Ohio River, Cincinnati sparkled in the night, but Deke only had eyes for Kelsey. She hadn't spoken for a while. "Kelsey, are you still awake over there?" When she turned her head toward him, he reached across the central console to took her hand.

Kelsey and gave his hand a little squeeze. She smiled and said, "I'm awake. I'm just so relaxed." She let her head fall against the head rest and covered an enormous, jaw-cracking yawn with her free hand.

"Uh, oh," Deke said. "I saw that yawn. This date must be a real snooze. I guess I'm gonna have to think of something to keep you awake."

Kelsey turned her head as Deke leaning toward her with a hungry look in his eyes. She closed her eyes and felt his lips land on her mouth with authority. He released her hand and cradled her face in his strong, work-roughened hands. When his tongue licked her bottom lip, she opened her mouth and sought his tongue with hers. Kelsey's nipples beaded and , rubbed against the front of her shirt, like little flowers reaching for the sun. She reached for his chest and dug her fingers into his granite hard pectorals. Deke flexed his chest muscles and grunted as he slid his hands from her face, down her shoulders and behind her back to pull her closer. Unfortunately, the central console of his truck kept Kelsey from plastering herself against Deke's body, but she turned her upper torso as much as possible within the confines of the seat belt and the luxuriously cushioned front seat.

Deke released his seat belt then popped hers, freeing them both to move even closer to each other in the dim confines of the truck cab. Kelsey pulled her legs up an kneeled on her seat, angling her body toward Deke's. She wrapped one arm around his massive upper back and rested the other elbow by his shoulder so that she could run her hand through his soft black hair. Deke reached around her waist and put both of his massive paws on her ass, giving her cheeks a tight squeeze. As his lips broke apart from hers, he hummed in pleasure, nuzzling his way toward the vee in her sweater and her aching breasts. When his lips finally reached her cleavage, Kelsey's head dropped back and she moaned again. Her breasts were so swollen that the cups of her bra felt tight. She craved his touch there. Deke mumbled as he tried to maneuver his mouth inside her bra., "I really want to strip this sweater off and suck on those little nipples of yours that are poking a hole into my chest right now."

Deke's honest passion was something Kelsey had never experienced before, but it totally turned her on. He was so raw and honest with his reactions that Kelsey felt like the sexiest woman alive. It was a powerful feeling and that power was making her bold. She surprised herself when she said, "Then you should probably take it off of me." Deke didn't need any further coaxing. He put his hands under the band of the cashmere sweater and lifted the garment over her breasts. He roughly cupped her breasts through her red lace bra and growled when he spotted the front closure. With one quick flick of his thumb, he released the little toggle snap. Her bra cups flew to the side and her tender breasts fell into his palms. He began to roll her nipples between his middle and ring fingers as he kneaded her swollen mounds. Kelsey just moaned with desire and rubbed her hands over his face and into his hair. Deke must have taken her reaction as a sign to continue the assault on her breasts with his tongue. When Deke licked her nipples and then began to lightly bite and suck on the sensitive tips, Kelsey's body began to vibrate with desire. She was almost delirious with the need to feel his mouth on the rest of her body. When Deke released her nipple with an audible pop, she yanked on his hair until her looked up at her. "Take me home!" she demanded, her chest heaving. "Please! I want to see you naked and I'm too old to make out in a car."

Deke's breath caught for a moment and then he growled at her, "You sure, Baby? Because if you let me into your front door tonight, I am gonna have you naked. I want you so much I think that the zipper in these jeans has made a permanent indentation on my cock. If you don't want me to make love to you, you had better tell me now." She could tell that he was totally serious about wanting to have sex with her, but she also knew that she could trust him to stop right now, if she changed her mind.

Kelsey gave his hair a little tug and said, "I have never been so sure of anything in my life. Let's go." She climbed off Deke's lap and back across the truck's console to her own seat. Kelsey grabbed her sweater and pulled it back on before grabbing her bra and shoving it into her purse. She buckled up and reached for the hand that Deke was holding out to her. "Let's go!"

Deke rested his forehead on the steering wheel and blew out a deep breath. He looked over at the disheveled beauty sitting in the passenger seat and grinned. "It's a good thing you put that sweater back on, Baby, or I'm liable to wreck the truck before we get there. Buckle up and hang on. We may get pulled for speeding."

Deke managed to back the truck out and then drive to Kelsey's little house without letting go of her hand. He made little circles on her palm with his thumb. When Deke parked in front of her place, she didn't wait for him to open her door, but released the seat belt, jumped to the sidewalk, and practically ran to her front door, digging the keys out of her purse as she went.

By the time she reached the front porch, Deke was right behind her, wrapping his arms around her waist and nibbling the side of her neck. Her hands shook as she unlocked the front door, but the locks finally turned and she practically fell into the entry hall in her rush to get Deke naked.

She stumbled in, dropped her purse and keys on the little table by the door and turned to meet Deke's lips as he slammed the door shut. They only broke their lip lock long enough to pull Kelsey's red sweater over her head for the second time that night. Deke's shirt was a button-up that immediately became a button-off when Kelsey ripped it open in her haste to get her hands onto that rock-hard chest. She moaned as she felt the muscles covered in a thick pelt of black chest hair. All she could do was pet his pectoral muscles in big round circles as the temptation of running her hand through his cuddly chest hair distracted her. As Deke toed-off his slip-on loafers, he grabbed her hands and moved them down to the waist band of his jeans. "How about you help me with these?"

Kelsey inhaled sharply and almost became dizzy from Deke's wood and citrus scent. She laid her forehead against his breastbone and kissed his chest as she fumbled with the button fly on his jeans. She had only gotten the first two rivets open when his jeans became loose enough to shove down his lean hips. Kelsey pushed her left hand into the waistband of his gaping denim and rubbed the thick cock trying to fight its way out of his black briefs. Deke's deep groan spurred her to tuck her hand inside the cotton briefs and grip his hot, engorged member.

Kelsey dropped to her knees and licked Deke's cockhead, humming at the musky pre-cum that was gathered at the slit. With the hand not full of Deke's throbbing erection, she finished opening his fly, then released his cock long enough to pull his briefs and pants down his legs before she gripped the massive rod with both hands and took the mushroom head into her mouth.

Deke's hands flew to Kelsey's hair and he thrust his hips gently toward her warm, wet mouth. "Kelsey, oh my god, Baby! God, your mouth feels so good. Suck it, Baby....oh, yeah....just like ..." Deke's voice faded away and all he could do was moan. Kelsey's mouth slid up and down the top half of Deke's cock as her two fists gripped him and rubbed up and down. Deke wound a hand into Kelsey's hair and pulled his cock from her mouth. Kelsey looked up with a mixture of dazed lust and confusion. "Baby, you've got to stop."

"Why? Am I doing it wrong?" Kelsey asked. Her face got pink with embarrassment and uncertainty.

"Oh, Hell NO! You were doing it so right that the evening almost ended with me coming in that hot little mouth of yours! I don't want our first time to be one-sided, Honey. I want to get you out of the rest of those clothes and get some place more comfortable so that we can make this last." Deke pulled her to her feet. He popped the button on her jeans and lowered the zipper while he kissed her with almost violent passion. As he pushed her jeans and her little red panties to the floor, he thrust his tongue in and out of her mouth, the same way she hoped he would soon be sliding his cock into her wet pussy.

Leaving a pile of clothing in the entryway, Deke hoisted a warm and naked Kelsey into his arms and gently slapped her ass. "Which way to the nearest bed?"

Kelsey smiled and wrapped her arms around Deke's neck.

"Down the hall, second room on the right," she answered. She was too excited about being held by such a delicious specimen of manhood to worry about whether or not she had actually made her bed. Hopefully, within the hour, the bed would be completely trashed from their hot and spicy naked wrestling. At least it would if she had anything to say about it.

For the first in her life, Kelsey was giddy at the prospect of being with a man. She wasn't self-conscious about her body or her desires--she only felt the same anticipation that burned in every look Deke gave her. Never in her life had she been so turned on and so happy with a naked man. This put all of the mediocre joyless sex she had with her ex-husband to shame.

Deke almost ran with Kelsey in his arms. He passed her bedroom, almost entered the linen closet, stopped, turned on his heel, and returned to her bedroom without breaking their kiss. He stopped, oriented, and strode toward her king sized bed. He gave Kelsey a little toss that sent her bouncing onto the middle of the mattress and then launched himself next to her. Kelsey laughed out loud as Deke landed next to her and bounced a couple of times on her mattress. "What are you laughing at?" Deke demanded and proceeded to tickle Kelsey's sides. Kelsey squealed and laughed hysterically as she tried to wriggle away. "Don't you know you're not supposed to laugh at a naked man? It gives us a complex."

"Oh, I've seen you naked and you have *nothing* too complex to worry about," Kelsey quipped. The growl coming from Deke's chest was the only warning she got before he renewed his deadly tickling assault.

"Stop! Stop!" she shouted, laughing hysterically. "Uncle! I give!" Deke stopped, but pinned her wrists above her head and leaned over her face with a predatory smile. Kelsey, worn out from laughing, licked her lips and watched Deke's mouth. Was she actually cracking jokes with a naked man? Who was this happy, uninhibited woman and what had she done with frigid Kelsey? Well, wherever that poor girl was, the new and improved Kelsey hoped the old Kelsey stayed firmly in her past.

"Did you just suggest that I'm not complex enough for you? You think I don't have game?" Deke transferred both of her wrists to one massive paw and used his free hand to palm her breast and pinch her nipple. Kelsey made a token effort to break free, but Deke didn't budge.

"Did anyone ever tell you that you talk too much when you're naked?"

His answer was to swoop down and capture her lips in a kiss that would have melted her panties had she been wearing any.

When he came up for air, Deke said, "Just for that, I'm going to make you come two times before you get any of my "simple" equipment, young lady." He ran his hand down her torso and buried his fingers in her already soaked labia.

"You are mean! How did I not see how mean you are?" Kelsey attempted a pout, but failed when her thighs began to quiver from the pleasure his wicked fingers were providing. She wiggled until their bodies were aligned and nipped Deke's chest. She soothed the little bites with open mouth kisses until Deke began massaging her engorged clit. His figure eights made her lose concentration. She inhaled sharply when he slid his ring and pinky fingers into the opening of her vagina. The added stimulation sent her over the edge into orgasm. She keened her pleasure and slammed her thighs together, trapping his hand firmly in the zone that he had just set on fire.

Deke placed his mouth over her left nipple and blew warm air on the erect bud. "That's one," he whispered, as he shifted to her other breast and began to suck in earnest. He removed his hand from her pussy and caressed her stomach as he made his way up to her right breast. He alternated between pulling and twisting her nipple between his thumb and finger and massaging her breast. The contrast between the warm suction of his mouth and the sharp pinching worked Kelsey up toward another release. Every pull and biting sting on her nipples sent pulses of pleasure to her uterus. Her pussy clenched air. When the pleasure became too great, her second orgasm sent deep ripples through her lower body. Kelsey gasped as wave after wave of bliss relaxed every muscle in her body.

"Shit!' Deke stiffened. "My jeans...and the condoms...are in your hallway."

"I think I can help you out." Kelsey fumbled for her nightstand drawer, yanked it open and pulled out a brand new box of condoms. Deke took the box from her hand with a satisfied hum. She vaguely heard the rip of packaging and some rustling linens. Before she finished gasping about how amazing his game actually was, his lips locked onto hers with a deep, slow, wet kiss and he slid his thick cock into her still spasming pussy.

His moans of pleasure vibrated her mouth and his thrusts into her clenching body expanded the aftershocks from her most recent orgasm. Deke powered into her sensitive channel, losing his breath before reaching his own peak on a long, low moan.

CHAPTER THIRTEEN

As Kelsey lay quietly in Deke's arms, she sighed with pleasure.

"Was that a good sigh or a bad sigh?" Deke asked as he ran his fingertips up and down the arm that she had wrapped around his chest.

Kelsey snuggled her head more comfortably under Deke's chin and said, "It was a great sigh. I don't think I have ever enjoyed sex so much." Kelsey lifted her head a little and struggled to see Deke's face in the darkened room. "Maybe I'm not supposed to say that? I'm not really familiar with proper protocol after something like this," she said .

"Something like *this*?" Deke asked. "What do you mean something like this?"

"You know," Kelsey murmured, "a *thing*. A casual thing. Making blanket angels on the first date...Um..." Kelsey was at a loss.

Deke barked a laugh. "We are naked, after making mind-blowing love, and you don't know what the *protocol* is? How about you just say what you feel without worrying about what you *think* you are supposed to say."

"Well, then, thank you," Kelsey said.

Deke's laughter shook the bed, but he pulled Kelsey tighter. "You don't have to thank me, Honey, I was right there with you, enjoying the hell out of this *thing*, too."

"Well, I'm thanking you anyway," Kelsey said. "I spent years thinking I was no good at sex, but you just helped me learn that I *can* enjoy sex. For that, I am grateful."

Deke gently skimmed her arm. "Well, for what it's worth, I think you are more than just good at sex. I think you are phenomenal. I'm sorry that it has taken you this long to learn about yourself, but I'm truly humbled that you chose me to break your streak.'

Kelsey squirmed. She really didn't know what came after good sex in a relationship. Hell, she didn't even know if one date constituted a relationship. Wow, she had just put out on a first date! The old Kelsey would have been horrified, but the new, improved seize-the-day Kelsey, who had survived a lightning strike, performed a mental fist pump. Score! Still, what to do next with the man in her bed?

Kelsey stiffened in Deke's arms...Because he was so good at the sex thing, he obviously had had *a lot* of practice, right? That only made sense, since he was *so very, very good* at making love. Did she invite him to spend the night? Did they just go to sleep and wait to see what happened in the morning? Was she supposed to offer him a drink, or dared she initiate the next round of sexy time?

"I can hear the gears grinding in your head," Deke said. "What's the matter, Kels?"

Kelsey pulled out of Deke's embrace and sat up on the side of the bed. She rested her elbows on her knees and dropped her face into her hands. "I don't know what I'm supposed to do next," she declared. "I've never had a one night stand before." Kelsey moaned. "Oh my god, I don't even know if that's the wrong thing to call this!"

The bed dipped behind her. Deke scooted up to her back and wrapped his arms around her waist. His prickly beard rubbed her shoulder as he placed little kisses on her temple. "Hey, Honey. Don't worry so much," he said. "We don't have to call this *anything* right now. We are just two consenting adults who really enjoyed our time together. It is no more and no less than that."

"So you don't think I'm easy because I put out on the first date?" she asked.

"Do you think I'm some kind of asshole because I got you into bed on the first date?"

"No!"

"Well, then," Deke said, "why would you judge yourself more harshly than you judged me? Just relax and enjoy our time together. There is no need for labels or judgments." Deke's little kisses slowly worked their way to the shell of her ear. His hands wandered to her breasts and began massaging. Kelsey moaned and turned into Deke's warm embrace.

"I'll tell you one thing that I definitely need right now," Kelsey mumbled in between kisses, "and that's a refresher course. What was that thing I was supposed to do with my tongue, again?"

"Here," Deke slid his mouth down her neck and worked his way toward the top of her smooth, hairless mound. "Allow me to demonstrate...." Deke spent the next few minutes showing her exactly how useful a tongue could be and rung two scorching hot orgasms from her before another round of delicious lovemaking. Afterward, they lay tangled and sweaty in each others' arms.

Kelsey gave a little giggle.

"What's so funny?" he asked.

"Nothing," she said as she patted his sculpted stomach. "I just remembered that I have to write a thank you note for something." She smiled and rolled over to snuggle up to the man who had made her Brazilian wax worthwhile.

CHAPTER FOURTEEN

Deke's telephone sounded an alarm at 5:30 a.m., waking both of them from a deep sleep. Deke groaned loudly and reached for the little black box making the huge obnoxious ringing noise.

"Good Morning , Honey I'm sorry about the early wake up, but I have to be at a building site to meet with a subcontractor at 6:00. He rolled out of bed and reached for his clothes. They looked none the worse for wear, despite having spent several hours laying in the front hallway, because they had both gathered their clothes in the middle of the night when they hit the kitchen for some water. All of that hot lovemaking was thirsty work!

Kelsey slowly got out of bed, grabbed a robe and made her way into the kitchen. She started coffee and toast while Deke showered, and scrambled eggs while he dressed. Deke wolfed his eggs and toast before Kelsey had begun to eat hers, apologized for having to run out the door, thanked her for the breakfast with a kiss, and gathered up his wallet, keys and phone. After a final scorching kiss goodbye, he promised to call her later. Kelsey leaned against the closed door with a deep sigh and a huge grin. By mid-morning, her cheeks ached from smiling. She was a modern woman having a mature, adult fling! She could do this...right? She could definitely handle entertaining nights out with a handsome man, followed by blazing hot lovemaking with no morning-after awkwardness.

Within couple of hours of Deke's goodbye kiss, Charlie arrived home full of energy and wild tales of scary movies and ghost stories.

Over the course of the morning, all of the Girls had called to get the scoop, but Kelsey hedged and hinted. She wanted to savor her time with Deke, and it seemed wrong to talk about it yet, even with her closest friends. She couldn't keep the smile out of her voice, though, so there were lots of cat calls and hissing, even as they congratulated her on taking the leap back into the dating pool.

Kelsey tried to concentrate on housework, but her mind kept drifting back to her blissful night. She gave up on cleaning after she sprayed hair spray on her dresser instead of furniture polish and figured she could distract herself with work. She deleted every third word in every document she tried to write because her mind kept defaulting to Deke and how much fun they had together, both clothed and naked. It wasn't just the mind-blowing orgasms that had her brain pushing rewind on her memories. She kept chuckling over Deke's sense of humor and recalling how he seemed able to put everyone around him at ease. She couldn't stop grinning at the way he had assuaged her "morning after" jitters by making her feel powerful and respected... and sexy as hell. Most surprising, though, was the warm tingle she got every time she remembered how Deke had stood up to Brad The Bastard before their date had begun. Kelsey shook her head and tried to focus. That man was dangerous to her peace of mind and her productivity.

By the middle of the afternoon, she had managed to complete three projects before a knock sounded on the door. Cat and Lyssie stopped by on their way home from shopping to have a cup of coffee and get the details that she had refused to disclose over the phone earlier. Kelsey recognized their determined expressions, so she let them in and prepared for the inquisition. As she made a fresh pot of coffee, her friends settled around the cozy oval oak table in Kelsey's eat-in kitchen and stared at her until she began to spill the details of her date with Deke. Since Charlie was busy playing in his backyard sandbox, well out of ear shot, she figured she could give them all of the details without traumatizing her child. She started out by assuring them both that she had enjoyed the date, how much fun it had been to meet Deke's family and extolling how easy he was to talk to. She described how handsome he had looked and how he had paid such close attention to her when she was talking about her work and her family, showing such genuine interest. She tried to throw them off of the scent of her inability to stop thinking about Deke's mad nakey-time skills by casually mentioning that he had spent the night, but would not give them any details about the sex, except to say that it was mind blowing. Lyssie and Cat just listened and kept making little noises of encouragement, without really commenting. They both just sat, with skeptical looks and let her keep babbling about how wonderful and nice and handsome and polite and hot Deke was... As Kelsey waxed on about how much she really liked Deke and how smart and caring he was, she moved from the table to the counter to get the coffee pot. She started to fill everyone's coffee cup when she caught her two friends sharing concerned looks across the kitchen table that spoke volumes.

"What?" Kelsey finally asked.. "Why are you two looking at me like that?"

"Honey, we are just a little concerned," Cat began. "This was the first date you've had in a really long time and you seem a little *too* excited. Don't get us wrong...you *should* be excited." Cat raised her hands, palms out, in a gesture meant to calm the storm brewing on Kelsey's face. "But you already sound like a girl with a Major League Crush. We ...well, we don't want you to read too much into it."

"Not that you are," Lyssie rushed to reassure her, "but we just don't want to see you get hurt. You have a big heart and we don't want to see you hand it over too soon and get it trampled on."

Kelsey plunked the coffee pot down on the table and practically fell into her chair, shoving her face into her hands to cover her rapidly pinkening cheeks. "I'm pathetic, aren't I?" she moaned. "I have totally read more into this than there is and I made a fool of myself." She put her head down on her arms and moaned into the scarred wood. Cat and Lyssie both protested.

'No, not pathetic, Kelsey' Lyssie said.

"I'm sure you were absolutely cool and casual or Deke would have chewed his arm off to sneak out of your bed without waking you this morning," Cat said, patting Kelsey's arm. "You would have known if you'd spooked him."

Lyssie said, "Exactly! You obviously played it perfectly last night. We are just worried that you don't get too attached too soon." .

Kelsey raised her head. Her embarrassed blush started to fade and a determined look took its place. "You're right. I am totally over thinking this. I need to lower my expectations. Last night was good...no *great.* If Deke calls me again, I will be happy for a repeat, but he is not the only hot, single man around. Maybe he never wants to take me out again. Maybe he does. Either way, I am still a great catch and any man would be lucky to have me. After all, I have just started this dating thing and I definitely deserve to see what's out there."

"Exactly," Cat said. "You don't need a permanent relationship right now. You just want to have some fun, right?"

"Right," Lyssie agreed. "Don't get too attached to Deke. Remember, you'll be working for him. Things would get awkward if you stopped dating while you were still working for his company."

Kelsey screwed her face up into an "I just sucked a lemon" face and cringed. "You are absolutely right. *Awwwkward!* I just need to chalk this up to a really good re-entry into the dating scene... I mean, a really, *really* good re-introduction, and move on. Dating Deke is probably not a good idea. After all, I need to get into the C&Y offices to see if I can find information on Brad's funding, and I don't want to jeopardize that by coming on too strong on a personal level."

Kelsey squared her shoulders and called on her inner courage. She just needed the strength to remain friendly with Deke, but to decline any more dates with him. She wasn't even sure that he was going to ask. He had left this morning without setting up another time to see her. But if he did ask, she would politely decline. She didn't want to hurt his feelings, so she would explain that she had a policy against dating clients. Since he owned his own business, she was sure he would understand. She just had to stand her ground and distance herself so that she didn't get hurt. After all, hadn't Deke been the one who said their *thing* was whatever she wanted it to be?

Lyssie and Cat headed out the door after extracting Kelsey's promise to join The Girls for drinks on Thursday.

She convinced Charlie to take a nap with her in the early afternoon, under the premise of watching a movie with her. He fell asleep within minutes and Kelsey finally had a moment to savor her deliciously sore muscles and remember the steamy lovemaking that had kept her awake half the night. She drifted off to sleep remembering the warmth of Deke's body pressing her down into the mattress.

Half an hour later, she was rudely yanked from a delicious dream by the buzz of her cell phone on the nightstand.

"Hello," she mumbled..

"Hello, Beautiful," Deke's hypnotic voice said. "Do you miss me yet?"

Kelsey grinned and stretched her sleep-stiffened body. As she wiggled back into a comfortable divot in her memory foam mattress, she couldn't help the breathy little sigh that escaped. "Hmmmm...who is this again," Kelsey giggled.

"You already forgot, huh? I guess I'll have to finagle a repeat performance to make a more lasting impression. Are you free right now?" he asked.

Kelsey gave a little laugh. "Oh, I'm free, but I don't think you want to put that particular show on in front of my six-year-old, do you?"

"Well, that particular performance might be geared more toward a mature, female audience, so I guess it will have to wait until we're alone." he chuckled. "Hey, I discussed your services with my partner, Eli, and he is just as excited as I am. I showed him your website proposals this afternoon and he picked the same one that my mom did. I think that means we are ready to start. "

Kelsey's smile broadened. "Wow! That was fast. I guess I *am* just that good!" She laughed. "Really, I'm excited. I can absolutely get started this week. How is Monday?"

Deke hesitated a second and replied, "I was actually kind of hoping we could get together tonight. I'd really like to see you. We don't have to talk about business. We can grab some dinner and see a movie or something. Do you like action movies?"

Kelsey panicked. She had enjoyed her night with Deke,

but after her talk with the girls, she needed to reel in her feelings...keep it casual...cool. Hadn't they agreed this would be a casual thing? Kelsey didn't have extensive experience with flings, but she was pretty sure that being part of a casual sexual relationship did *not* involve seeing the other person every night. What was Deke doing? She gave herself a mental shake. Stop it! Slow means slow!

"Deke, I can't tonight," Kelsey said. "I mean, I really appreciate the offer, but I am going to spend tonight with Charlie. We have big plans involving animated car movies and popcorn. Thanks, anyway, though."

"Hey, I don't mind a night-in. How about I stop by the store and load up on snacks and join you for movie night? I can watch anything," he finished.

Kelsey hesitated. Part of her wanted to see Deke, but the more practical side thought this was supposed to be a fling and didn't want to seem too eager. *Keep it light*, she thought, *be cool.*

"No," she said, trying to keep her tone light. "I would not wish A Hillbilly Talking Tow Truck on anyone," she said with a small laugh. "How about we set up a time to all meet on Monday? Check your calendars and let me know what time would be good for me to come to your office." Kelsey worried that she had blown her chances with Deke, both personal and professional.

"Okay," he answered quietly. "I'll give you a call tomorrow to set up a time."

"Okay, great!" Kelsey said in too chipper a voice. "I'll talk with you tomorrow, then! Enjoy your evening."

"You, too," Deke said. "Goodbye."

"Bye!" Kelsey hung up the phone and cringed. She could tell by Deke's tone that he hadn't expected her to blow him off.

She had to put some distance between them, didn't she?

She just hoped that her friends' advice was right and that Deke was not her only shot at true love. She sighed deeply and returned to the family room where Charlie was bouncing on the couch, excitedly waiting for her to start the movie. Kelsey smiled. *This* is what is important. My son has to come first and I have to figure out a way to make Brad help support him so that our child can have the best start in life that we can give him. If I have to sacrifice a few nights of hot sex so I can secure his future, then that is *exactly* what I, as a good mother, should do....right?

CHAPTER FIFTEEN

Deke hung up his cell phone and stared out of the window of his kitchen. Well, *that* was unexpected. He had rushed through work with a huge smile on his face in anticipation of spending the evening with Kelsey. True, he hadn't nailed anything down with her before he left this morning, but they had parted on good terms. Or so he thought. They had hit it off so well, he thought they had skipped all the preliminary dating mumbo jumbo and gone right to the part where they knew they had something good and wanted to give it a go. Obviously, he had assumed too much.

Kelsey had actually blown him off for the entire rest of the weekend by telling him that she would meet with him on Monday. Maybe he had done something to spook her. Had he come on too strong?

Deke knew that Kelsey was not hung up on her ex, so what could it be? Was she back to feeling guilty for hitting the sheets with him so soon after meeting? Deke's hand curled into a fist. It better not have been something her asshole ex had said. If that little bastard had come back and threatened her again, he would bust his face, client or not.

He stood at the kitchen sink, sipped a beer and wondered what he had done to screw this up. When his phone rang, he looked at the display, hoping it was Kelsey, but it was his mom.

"Hey, Momma. What's up?" Deke asked.

"Hi, Honey! How's your Saturday treating you?" his mom asked.

"Well, it was fine until a few minutes ago, but now I'm not so sure. How is everything down that way?"

"We're fine, just fine. I really enjoyed meeting your new lady friend last night. She was a doll, and so talented!" Phyllis exclaimed. "Those websites were really neat. She seems to really get you and Eli. Tucker really liked her too. I was actually calling because we wondered if you and Kelsey would like to go with Tucker and me to the fair tonight. Tucker has a pecan pie in the Pie Event and we want to scope out the competition. The weather is going to be nice, and we are closing at five since everyone around here will be at the fairgrounds anyway."

"Sorry, Momma, but Kelsey and I aren't going out tonight. In fact, I just called to see if we could get together and she pretty much blew me off." .

"Dang it, Deacon! I really liked her! What did you do to tick her off?"

Deke made a face. "Gee, thanks, Momma! How do you know that *I* did something? I was pretty surprised she said no, actually. I can't think of anything I did to upset her," Deke said, trying to remember any awkward moments or signs that Kelsey had given that showed she was uncomfortable. "In fact, I thought last night was one of the best dates I have ever had and I thought she felt the same. I have no idea what happened between the time I left her house and when I just called."

"What did she say when you asked why she was canceling your plans?" Phyllis asked.

"Well, we didn't actually *have* any pre-arranged plans. I just felt so comfortable with her that I thought she felt the same way and we would just go with the flow. She didn't say she had anything special lined up for tonight when we talked earlier."

"Deacon Connelly, what in the world makes you think that a beautiful, smart, classy woman like Kelsey is just sitting around waiting for you to call her to make last minute plans on a Saturday night?" Phyllis laughed. "Son, women like that don't sit around and wait for anyone, even handsome, nice boys like you. They get on with their lives. If you want to spend time with Kelsey, you have to *ask* her to save some time for you."

His mom was absolutely right, Deke thought. He felt kind of sheepish for assuming that Kelsey was going to be available this weekend when he hadn't mentioned seeing her again. He could have smacked himself for not nailing something down with her. He didn't think that she would be mollified by the fact that he was too distracted by her naked body to think clearly, either. Damn, he was a fool!

"I'm sure you're right, Momma. When I called, she said that she was going to stay home and watch movies with her little boy. I said I would come over and watch whatever and just hang out, but she shut me down."

"Son, if Kelsey is a mom, you are going to have to work a lot harder than you are used to in order to get anywhere with her. A good mother will always put her child first, and she will be very careful about personal relationships that could affect him. Have you met her little boy yet?"

"No," Deke answered. "Last night was only our first real

date, unless you count coffee earlier in the week, but that was really a business meeting."

"Well," Phyllis said, "don't be surprised if she keeps you at arm's length until you can prove that you are serious about her and not just out for a good time. If you haven't met her son, I would have been shocked if she had said yes when you asked to hang out with them, especially at her home."

"What do you mean? I would never do anything to hurt a kid!"

"Deacon, it has nothing to do with whether or not you mean to hurt her boy. Kids don't understand how complicated adult relationships are, and Kelsey is probably very careful who she lets into her son's life so he doesn't get attached to someone who isn't sticking around. If she let you hang around with them, especially this early in your relationship, that little boy would be just as hurt as Kelsey if things didn't work out," Phyllis explained. "Why do you think I never brought anyone around you after your daddy died? I had plenty of dates, but none of them were going to stick, so I kept you and your brother out of it."

"I get it." Deke sighed. "I really clicked with her, Momma. I'm just going to have to figure out how I can get her to give us a chance."

"You're a smart boy, Deke," Phyllis said. "I know you will figure out a way. If you want something badly enough, you always do."

"Thanks, Momma. Hey, let me know if Tucker wins so I can stop by the fair tomorrow for a piece of that pie!"

"Will do, son. Take care." Phyllis hung up and Deke slid his phone onto the counter-top charging station. Since he wasn't going out tonight, he might as well charge his phone.

He grabbed his beer and headed to the living room to flip through channels on his ridiculously large, ninety-inch, flat screen television. He loved to watch professional hoops on the big screen. There weren't any professional basketball teams in the area, and this was the closest he could get to a live event. If he couldn't spend the evening with Kelsey, he would stay in and come up with a plan to woo the pants right off that little lady.

Yep, he smiled and took a long swig of lager, she wasn't going to know what hit her.

CHAPTER SIXTEEN

When Kelsey woke on Sunday morning, the sun was shining, birds were chirping and she wore a huge smile. Even if she couldn't see him every day, nothing in the dating handbook said she couldn't dream about the Delicious Deacon Connelly. Last night's nocturnal visitation had been epic. Who knew that finding the right man could make your days bright and your nights better, even if he came only in her dreams? Kelsey felt recharged after her early night with Charlie and wanted to do something fun with him. Yesterday, she had picked up half a dozen blueberry muffins on the way home from the movie rental kiosk. While they happily munched away at their decadent breakfast, she glanced through the Around Town section of the newspaper.

Under Sunday Events, a paragraph mentioned that the county fair was opening this weekend. Now, that sounded like a really great thing to share with Charlie! Her childhood experience with anything rural had been an annual hayride at the local pumpkin patch. She had never visited a county fair, but these days, she was all about new experiences, and a trip to the fair would be fun. Bucket List experience...ACTIVATE!

"Hey, Buddy, how about heading to a fair today?" Kelsey watched Charlie's eyes go round with excitement.

"Do they have rides and horses and stuff?" he asked, practically vibrating in his seat.

"I think so," she said. "I know they have games and funnel cakes and cotton candy, so it will be fun no matter what!"

"Oh, YEAH! Cotton candy!" Charlie wiggled and chanted, "Cotton candy! Cotton candy!" with the enthusiasm only a six-year-old could muster.

Kelsey laughed, shook her head, and dusted blueberry muffin crumbs off Charlie's face.

"Okay, Pal. Get dressed and let's go!"

It took twenty-five minutes and a couple of wrong turns for Kelsey and Charlie to find Simon County Fair's giant field full of colorful tents. The rutted field used as parking for the fair did its unlevel best to destroy her car's undercarriage, but Kelsey found a narrow opening between two giant pickup trucks and parked her little Honda Accord. She and Charlie locked up and headed for the big sign that said, "Welcome." Charlie practically bounced as they neared the sights and sounds of the county's annual celebration of all things agricultural. Heavenly smells of roasting meat and burnt sugar tickled their noses as they strolled through the first row of tents. There were all of the carnival games that she had seen in TV shows, like the milk bottle game and balloon darts with the prizes of giant stuffed animals in garish colors. Charlie thought it was all fabulous! He wanted to play every game, but Kelsey pulled him by the hand, promising they would return and play their favorite games after they had seen everything.

They turned a corner at the end of the row of game tents and Kelsey heard someone call her name. She stopped and looked around, finally meeting the lime green gaze of the smiling man making his way across the crowded games midway toward her. In that moment, Kelsey forgot that she was supposed to be playing it cool and keeping her distance. She smiled at the sheer pleasure of seeing him and remembered how it felt to be held in his strong arms. Deke stopped beside her and slipped his arm around her waist for a quick one-armed hug. He kissed her chastely on the cheek and said, "Hey there! Imagine running into you here!"

Kelsey didn't have a chance to answer before Charlie tugged her left hand and asked, "Mommy, who is this?"

CHAPTER SEVENTEEN

Deke released her waist, squatted, and held out a massive paw to Charlie.

"Hi, there! I'm Deke. You must be Charlie."

Charlie put his small hand into Deke's larger one, shook it solemnly and said, "Nice to meet you."

"Charlie," Kelsey began, "Deke is the man who helped me when I got hurt during the storm."

Charlie's eyes rounded. "You're the hero! Wow! Thanks for helping my mom! She got struck by lightning, but she didn't get any super powers." He gave Deke an assessing look and asked, "Did you get any? Mommy and her friends said you looked like Thor's brother Loki and I think they're right. Do you have a big hammer? Can I see it? You should use it to hit that game where you use the big hammer to try to ring the bell. I bet you'd totally win! Do you wanna go play with me?" Deke appeared a little overwhelmed.

"Charlie, I'm sure Deke is here with his friends and their feelings would get hurt if Deke left them to come and play with you," Kelsey said gently.

Deke stood and said in a disappointed tone, "You know what, I don't think I got any super powers, either."

Charlie gave him the supremely disappointed look that only a six-year-old can master, complete with slumped shoulders and sad eyes.

"I do have a hammer, though, because I build things in my job. I'd really like to play some games with you, if your mom says it's okay. I came by myself, so I won't hurt anybody's feelings." Deke looked over at Kelsey and noticed her slightly exasperated look. So, she thought her kid would scare him away, huh? Well, he may not be an actual superhero, but he had been a six-year old boy once and he knew what they liked. If his mom was right and the key to gaining Kelsey's trust was to show that he would be a good addition to her son's life, then Operation Charm the Pants Off Kelsey was ON!

He sensed Kelsey's reluctance to have him join them, but he wasn't taking no for an answer. He was not above bribery. At the fair, all was fair in love and war. He looked down at Charlie, then over at Kelsey and rubbed his hands together in anticipation. If there was one thing he remembered about being a six-year-old boy, it was their inherent inability to resist junk food, *especially* if their moms thought it was horrible. "Let's go get some cotton candy and play games!"

Bulls Eye!

Charlie's eyes got huge and he started jumping up and down, pulling on Kelsey's arm.

"Can we, Mom? Can we?" Charlie pleaded with his best puppy dog eyes. "Pleeeeeeeeease, Mom? Come on!"

Kelsey narrowed her eyes at Deke, but he smiled innocently.

"Yeah," Deke said, grinning, "come on, Mom!"

Deke saw the moment Kelsey conceded defeat. Her

shoulders relaxed and she smiled like she knew she was beaten.

"Okay, we can go with Deke," Kelsey said, but when Charlie turned and started to run back toward the games, "BUT you can NOT run away from us! You have to hold our hands and behave yourself or we won't play. Got it?"

"I got it!" Charlie agreed. "Come on, Deke! I'll show you where the big bell is! Then we can shoot water at the ducks and smack the moles and...," Charlie continued on, excitedly, as he walked between Deke and Kelsey, holding onto each of their hands and impatiently tugging them along. He pulled them toward the first game and danced from foot to foot as they waited in line. Charlie walked a few feet away to the front to check out the prizes and Kelsey looked over at Deke to assess his sincerity about spending the day with her and her rambunctious son.

"Fancy meeting you here today. What are you doing here?" She asked. "Hoping to put your superhero powers to work by saving someone from the top of a stuck Farris wheel?"

Deke snorted, "Funny girl! No, I came by to try to hook up with Tucker and my mom. Tucker entered his pecan pie in the Pie Contest and I wanted to show some support. Besides," he said slyly, "I didn't have anything else to do, since the beautiful woman I had *hoped* to spend the weekend with totally blew me off." Deke smiled slightly and raised one eyebrow, inviting her to explain.

Kelsey held his gaze, her expression a mix of embarrassment and stubbornness. "Look, Deke, I had a really good time Friday night—"

"...and Saturday morning, if I recall. At least, four really good times, but who's counting?" Deke intoned, waggling his eyebrows and laughing. Kelsey blushed and raised her hand, palm out, to stop his joking.

"Okay, you've made your point, but I just got out of a really crappy marriage and I have a son to worry about. I am just not ready to jump back into a relationship. Charlie is impressionable and has no idea that you aren't just a "friend" like the Girls are to me or his little buddies are to him. He will accept you into his heart and it would really hurt us--I mean *him*--if you suddenly stopped hanging around because things didn't work out between you and me. You can't jump in and start a relationship with him and then leave me holding the bag when it gets too heavy for you. How am I going to explain why you don't come around anymore when I can't even figure out how to tell him why his dad is never around anymore?" Kelsey was getting more agitated with every word.

Deke put his hands on her shoulders. She was stiff to the touch, but he rubbed her upper arms in small circles until she relaxed and her breathing calmed.

"Hey, now, Honey. It's okay." Deke rubbed her shoulders and waited for Kelsey to look up and meet his gaze. "I understand! You don't want to do anything that could confuse Charlie. You are a good momma. I know that, but I also know that I am a good man, too. I wouldn't do anything to hurt either one of you. Let's just have some fun right now. Charlie doesn't need to know that I'm anything other than your friend. After today, I won't try to invite myself over or bribe him to get into your good graces and I'll let you take the lead." He lifted a hand to cradle her cheek. "Just don't shut me out."

Kelsey's expression softened and she smiled slightly. "Okay, but we are just friends having fun at the fair, okay? That's all I can handle today."

"You got it!" Deke released Kelsey just as Charlie came bounding back.

"We gotta win the Penguin!" he exclaimed. "It's my

favorite animal! Do you know that penguins live in the North Pole *and* the South Pole? Isn't that cool? Some of them even live where it isn't cold at all...."

CHAPTER EIGHTEEN

The rest of the afternoon flew by in a whirlwind of laughter and cotton candy. Kelsey could not remember ever having so much fun, and Charlie was having the time of his life. Charlie's running commentary of everything he had ever learned in his life was as hilarious and satisfying as the games, the junk food and the rides. Deke and Charlie even competed in the Fishing Frenzy, where Deke taught Charlie how to put a worm on his hook and cast a line. They cheered at the four-inch blue gill Charlie caught. He released the fish, but not before he got a memorial picture and a certificate to commemorate his momentous first catch. The three of them bet on the frogs in the Frog Jumping Contest, and groaned at the amount of hot dogs the winner of the Hot Dog Eating Contest consumed. Kelsey tried to talk Deke into entering the Arm Wrestling Contest, but he refused. Charlie said he understood, with Deke being a hero and all, it probably wouldn't be fair to the rest of the contestants. Deke nodded solemnly and told Charlie that he had the makings of a great sidekick. Charlie, of course, agreed.

As the afternoon wound down, they made their way to the prepared foods and produce barn in time for the judging. They located Phyllis and Tucker, who made a big deal about what a handsome boy Charlie was and thoroughly admired his fish catching certificate and the penguin that Deke had won for him at the Balloon Water Gun Shootout.

Tucker's pie won second place and they cheered as he accepted his ribbon. The five of them then made their way to the barbeque tent and ate dinner seated around a picnic table.

They watched the sun go down as they listened to a local band play country music. While the adults were still going strong, Kelsey could tell that Charlie was winding down. He got petulant about not getting a second wand of cotton candy, so Kelsey told everyone that they were going to call it a night. She gathered up their things and accepted Deke's offer to carry a very tired Charlie to her car. Since Deke made the wise decision of offering Charlie a piggyback ride instead of carrying him like a baby, Charlie enthusiastically agreed. Kelsey wished goodnight to Phyllis and Tucker and then led the way toward the grassy field where she had parked.

After stumbling in the dark on the uneven ground a couple of times, Kelsey accepted Deke's arm as support. While they searched for the car, Kelsey had a hard time remembering why she was supposed to keep her distance from the charming contractor. He had patiently answered Charlie's five million questions as though he spoke to a person twice his age. Brad had *never* made Charlie feel so important and, she had to admit, she would never have lasted all day, or participated in half as many activities, without Deke there to help.

When Deke's strong arm kept her from hitting the ground as she stumbled on the rutted turf for the third time, she stopped for a second and caught her breath. For the first time, Kelsey realized, she had actually spent the day with a man who had helped her entertain her son, instead of competing with the boy for attention. Not once had Deke interrupted Charlie's ramblings about every new thing he saw or told him he couldn't try something because he might get dirty. It was so sexy watching the big man be so patient with her little boy. Kelsey could tell that Deke was genuinely having fun.

Deke had opened a whole new world to them. She owed him a debt of gratitude….*again*. She felt a sense of obligation to Deke, but it was more than that. This man, that she barely knew, had not only saved her life, but had given Charlie one of the best days of his young life. He was so handsome, but he was also funny and patient with the million and one questions that her kid threw at him all day. He was smart, but didn't take himself too seriously. Kelsey felt herself feeling so deeply for a virtual stranger, albeit one that she had seen naked. She already felt like she knew Deacon Connelly better after a few weeks than she had ever know her ex-husband in all of the years she had been married. It was disconcerting to feel so much for a man she barely knew. How could she trust these feelings or trust herself after being so blindsided by the man she had spent so many years thinking she could trust?

At last, they located her little sedan. Kelsey unlocked the doors with her key fob while Deke carefully slid Charlie down his back onto the ground. Charlie grabbed Deke around the knees and gave him a tight squeeze. "Thanks for the fun day, Deke!"

"You are sure welcome, Little Man. Now, climb on in and buckle up." Deke ruffled Charlie's hair and held the back door open so Charlie could climb up into the back seat and put on his seat belt. With Charlie safely buckled in, Deke closed the back door and turned to Kelsey, who had lingered nearby watching them.

She looked down at the ground and then up at Deke. “You sure make it hard not to like you, Mr. Connelly,” she said.

“Well, then,” Deke said as he reached for her hand and pulled her into a friendly hug, “quit trying so hard to dislike me, Mrs. Taggert.”

CHAPTER NINETEEN

Deke reeled Kelsey in for a goodbye hug and couldn't help wishing he could kiss her goodnight. Her soft expression each time she looked at her son made him crave her kiss, but he had agreed to slow things down in front of Charlie. Deke pulled her close and Kelsey raised her hands as if she meant to stop him from getting too intimate, but when her hands landed on his chest, she curled them into his pectoral muscles, almost as if she needed to hold on to something to steady herself, and she moaned softly. Deke's blood heated and his good intentions turned naughty. He lowered his head slowly, ready to stop if she made any gesture of disapproval, but her lips parted and he dropped his mouth over hers in a strong, deep kiss. He ran his tongue over her lower lip and she moaned again, opening wider. She massaged his chest in small circles as he wrapped his arms around her waist. He kissed her like and was drowning and she was fresh air. She returned the kiss with just as much passion. He moaned out loud, coming quickly back to reality when he heard someone knocking on the window beside them and giggling.

Kelsey broke their kiss, seeming to suddenly remember where they were, and gently, but firmly, shoved Deke's chest. He relaxed his hold and put some distance between their upper bodies but didn't release her. He intended to be a part of Kelsey's life, so Charlie might as well get used to shows of affection. God knew, he wasn't going to be able to keep his hands to himself.

They both turned to see the grinning face of her six year old peering through the car window and laughing hysterically. When Charlie started making kissy faces against the car window, Deke gave a little laugh and said, “I think we should table this discussion until we don’t have an audience.”

Kelsey looked from Charlie’s grinning face to Deke’s and shook her head. “Thanks a lot for spending the day with us. Charlie had a really good time,” she said.

“And what about Charlie’s momma?” Deke asked.

“Charlie’s mom had a good time too.” Kelsey smiled, “but I have to get him home now. Are we still on for going over the website changes with your partner tomorrow?” Kelsey asked as she opened the driver’s door and tossed her purse into the passenger seat.

“Absolutely,” Deke confirmed. “Why don’t you come by our office tomorrow around 10 a.m. We’ll have finished meeting with the subs by then and we’ll have time to talk.”

“Great. Sounds like a plan. Do you want me to drive you to your truck?” Kelsey asked.

Deke held the driver’s door open as Kelsey slid behind the wheel. She buckled her seat belt, rolled down the manual window, then closed the door firmly. “No, thanks, I’m just a couple rows over. Sweet dreams, Honey. Good night, Charlie!” Deke tapped the roof of Kelsey’s car twice with his knuckles and then backed away so she could pull out of her rutted parking spot. Deke caught Kelsey's eyes in her rearview mirror and smiled. Her eyes crinkled happily and she stuck her hand out of the window to give a little finger wave goodbye.

He grinned as he headed for his truck and home. Only twelve more hours before he saw her again. Mondays were definitely looking better.

CHAPTER TWENTY

Monday morning dawned as bright and sunny as Deke's smile. He allowed extra time to shave and dress, wanting to ensure that his powers of persuasion were fully loaded when Kelsey reached his office. He wanted her to see his professional side and be impressed by the business that he and Eli had built.

After meeting with the sub-contractors at his two busiest building sites, Deke hurried to the C&Y offices.

"Good Morning, Betty. How was your weekend?"

C&Y's long-time receptionist smiled from behind her tidy desk, "Morning, Deacon! You sure look nice today...hot lunch date?" she asked.

"Something like that," he responded. He dropped some paperwork off on her desk before heading to the office kitchen to start a fresh pot of coffee to go with the blueberry muffins from Kelsey's favorite coffee shop that he had picked up a few minutes ago. He kept peeking through the doorway of the kitchen through the reception area as ten o'clock rolled around, expecting Kelsey any minute. He didn't even mind the knowing smirk that his receptionist kept sending his way. After his eleventh trip from his office to the kitchen, he finally heard the front door open and tried to walk nonchalantly to stand near Betty's desk. Kelsey walked through the door and he felt such a surge of adrenaline when he spotted her smiling face crossing his threshold that he almost tripped over his own feet in an attempt to reach her before the door closed completely behind her. He grabbed the hand she extended for a handshake, hauled her close for a fierce hug and smiled into her hair when she laughed and said, "Good morning!"

"It is now," he declared. He gave her a final squeeze and released her. "Here, give me your bag." He tugged the nylon briefcase from Kelsey's hand and turned to meet the laughing gaze of the older woman standing behind the small reception desk. "This is Betty. She runs the place. Betty, this is Kelsey Taggart. She is going to get our files in order and fix our website."

Betty held out her hand."Good Lord, you found a saint!" Betty declared. "Welcome, Kelsey. I am happy to shake the hand of any woman brave enough to tackle that filing system. Please let me know if I can do anything to help."

"Thanks, Betty, it's nice to meet you, too." Kelsey shook the older woman's hand.

"Ok, let's head back to the conference room so I can show you where you'll be working," Deke said, placing his hand on her lower back to guide her through the office. "You can drop your things there and I'll give you the nickel tour." Once they reached the conference room behind Betty's reception desk, Deke slid the door closed took two long strides, grabbed Kelsey around the waist and hauled her against his chest for a kiss. Kelsey's initial muffled "oomph" of surprise turned into a moan as her lips softened and she returned his kiss. Deke gently broke their lip lock and sighed. "Now, *that's* the way you say good morning to a beautiful woman."

Kelsey laughed. "Is that the way you greet *all* the women you consider beautiful or...?"

“Nope. Only the ones I’ve seen naked."

She smiled at him from the circle of his arms. "Well, that’ll make it easy to spot your old conquests when we’re out in public!"

He snorted. "I guess you’ll have to go out with me again in order to test your theory."

"I suppose you're right," she said.

Deke gave a mental fist pump."Let's drop your stuff here and I’ll show you around,” Deke said. They dropped Kelsey’s purse and work bag on the conference room table and moved back to the hall. His tour of the one-story Craftsman home that he and his partner had renovated to become their headquarters began with the updated kitchen, followed by the bathroom, complete with granite shower stall and nickel fixtures. The conference room was the largest of the former home’s three bedrooms, with Deke and Eli’s offices occupying the two smaller bedrooms. All of the rooms, except the tiled kitchen and bathroom, sported gleaming hardwood floors. Deke and Eli had refinished them by hand, eager to preserve the original workmanship of the 80-year-old house. Heavy-duty Berber area rugs and carpet runners protected the floors from dirty work boots.

In the former living room, stairs allowed access to a converted attic. Deke led Kelsey up the curved staircase into an open concept loft that he and Eli used as a showroom. They had built shelves and counters along the walls creating enough storage space for all of the material samples without making the room feel crowded. On display were high-end fixtures and hardware samples that a potential homebuyer might want to see when designing the interior of their custom home. Skylights made the room bright. Deke could tell from the little noises of approval that Kelsey made that she was impressed with the space. He practically glowed with pride. Having your woman's approval was important to a man. Deke knew that Kelsey didn't expect more from him than some kind of fling. For him, she was much more than a way to pass the time. He could picture a future with her and Charlie. Kelsey deserved an equal partner in life. He had already shown her that they could be good in the bedroom. Now he just had to show her that they could be good in all other aspects of life, as well.

CHAPTER TWENTY-ONE

Kelsey had to admit that Deke surprised her... and impressed her. C&Y Construction's offices were very nice. Deke clearly took his work seriously, even if he seemed to never take himself too seriously. Listening to his overview of the work he and Eli had done to the building would proved to anyone that Deke was *much* more than just a pretty face...he was a talented professional.

As they made their way down the stairs and back to the conference room, Kelsey spotted a blond-haired man almost as big as Deke walking ahead of them into the kitchen. Their footsteps must have alerted him to their presence, because he stopped and shouted, "Hey, Man! I didn't know you were here this morning."

The stranger transferred a coffee mug from his right hand to his left and held out his empty hand to shake hers. Kelsey paused, for just a moment, to take in the man's striking beauty. He was over six feet tall with shoulders that seemed to go on forever and a face that could grace the cover of any magazine, even though he hadn't shaved in a couple of days. But his most stunning feature was a pair of the brightest blue eyes that Kelsey had ever seen. Surrounded by thick black lashes and eyebrows as blond as his longish, wavy hair, Kelsey felt like Eli's icy blue eyes looked directly into her soul. Those eyes sparkled with mischief.

"You must be Kelsey," the light-haired man said with a smile that made his eyes twinkle. "It's nice to meet you, finally. I'm Eli Yates." Kelsey shook the man's hand and smiled back.

"Hello! Thanks for the opportunity to present my designs to you. I hope to show you something that catches your eye," Kelsey said.

Eli's face lit with a grin. "Oh, I already see something I like. I'm sure the web designs will be nice too," he said. Eli's grin told her the man knew he was good looking and knew the ladies knew it, too.

"Oh, you are a smooth one, aren't you?" Kelsey chuckled.

"Well, that is something you will have to judge for yourself, Beautiful Kelsey."

She laughed, as Eli had intended, and tugged her hand out of his grip. She recognized by the gleam in his eye that he intended to mess with his buddy Deke. She would bet that his sexy smile worked on just about everyone. Interestingly enough, while Kelsey appreciated his rough masculine beauty, she didn't feel any sort of spark for Eli. Shaking his hand was nowhere near as exciting as an accidental brush against Deke. Kelsey looked from Eli's laughing eyes over to Deke's scowling face.

"Okay," Deke said, "that's enough of that! Kelsey is a professional, so save your flirting for those little ladies at the Permit Office. Let's head over to the conference room. Kels, would you like some coffee?"

"Yes, please," she answered. "Black."

"Two sugars, I remember," Deke said as he turned into the kitchen to get her drink.

Kelsey looked over at Eli, who was visibly trying not to laugh. "Why do I feel like a fire hydrant that just got marked by the resident dog?" she asked.

Eli burst out laughing. "Oh, Kelsey! Deke isn't going to know what hit him, is he?" Eli was still chuckling as he followed Deke and Kelsey into the conference room. Deke was holding two mugs of coffee in one hand and a small tray of muffins in the other. As they settled in, Deke passed her coffee and a muffin while she unpacked her computer and set up. While the laptop booted, she sipped her perfectly sweetened coffee, then handed each man a set of presentation documents containing her biography, curriculum vitae, a list of clients who had agreed to serve as references, and a complete list of all of her company's offerings. Since Kelsey did most of her business on a project-by-project basis, she included estimates of how much time an average project took so that potential clients had a good idea of cost. As someone who had always had to conduct her personal life within a budget, Kelsey tried hard to meet her client's expectations in her professional life as well.

Deke and Eli had few questions about her overview materials. Eli teased her for attending the University of Kentucky, since his favorite college team, the University of Louisville Cardinals, had soundly trounced UK's Wildcats in their most recent basketball match-up, but most of the conversation centered around specific plans Kelsey had for their business..

"You know, Eli, I am a little disappointed that you are a Cardinal's fan, since you didn't go to school there, but I guess I can still work with you," Kelsey laughed. "In fact, I think we should make a little wager."

"Oh, yeah?" Eli retorted. "What did you have in mind?"

"I will bet you two free hours of web design against two hours of handyman work at my house that Wildcats beat the Cards."

"Oh, we'll take that bet," Eli said, holding out his hand to shake on it. "I guess we had better find enough work around here to keep you busy for the next three weeks to make sure you are still here to pay up when you lose."

"I guess you will!" Kelsey retorted, shaking Eli's hand to seal their wager.

Next, Kelsey pulled up the website she had customized for C&Y. She had spent time Sunday night after getting Charlie to bed adding tweaks that Deke and Phyllis had mentioned on Friday night. Both Deke and Eli were impressed with the designs and, in the end, both chose the same design, so the project was approved and contracted before Kelsey finished her first cup of coffee. Not too shabby for a Monday morning!

"Now, that's the way I like to do business," she declared with a smile. "I can tell that you are both going to be easy to work with!"

"You say that now," Eli replied, "but you haven't seen our filing cabinet yet."

Deke rolled his eyes and said, "He's right. You might take one look and run right out of here." Deke stood, crossed the room, and opened a set of bi-fold doors. Inside, stacked in what could best be described as haphazard, were boxes upon boxes of paperwork. Few of the boxes had lids and only half were labeled.

"These are our project files. We used try to keep one project per box but some projects ran into several boxes. Some of our current projects got mixed in with finished jobs, so it's almost impossible to find anything in this mess." Deke ran his fingers through his hair. "What do you think? Is this something you can tackle?"

Kelsey tore her eyes away from the closet and looked at the men. They wore almost identical expressions of hopefulness and embarrassment. "Well, I guess you weren't just trying to get a date with me when you said you might need my help in the office. Looks like I got here just in time."

All three of them laughed.

"Does that mean you'll help us?" Deke asked.

"Oh, I'll help you. But when the bill comes, just remember how grateful you are right now."

Eli winked at her. "I have a feeling that it will be worth *every penny*."

CHAPTER TWENTY-TWO

Kelsey agreed upon a schedule that involved working at the C&Y offices for fifteen hours a week, starting in two days, until the filing system was organized. This was really all she could spare and still keep up with her other commitments. Deke and Eli were so grateful that she accepted the job that they promised to have the filing cabinets and office supplies she requested waiting for her on the first day of work. They even pulled all of the boxes out of the closets and set them on the table to make it easier for Kelsey to reach everything. There was certainly something to be said for having a big, strong man (or two) around.

Kelsey arrived at the C&Y office on Wednesday, energized and full of excitement. All of those butterflies danced in her stomach to celebrate the giant paper organization project ahead of her. At least, that's what she told herself. The lie flew out the window the moment Deke greeted her at the reception desk with a kiss on the cheek and a hot cup of perfectly sweetened coffee. She mentally sighed. She was excited to see Deke. Too excited.

Betty was on a call when Kelsey walked in, so she gave her a friendly smile and continued moving toward the boardroom. When Deke gently grabbed her arm as she walked past him and pecked her on the cheek, Betty just gave them both a knowing smile and looked away. She was not fooling anyone, including herself. She was a little rattled by the good morning kiss while she considered herself "at the office" but Deke's obvious joy at seeing her quickly replaced her discomfort with happiness to see him. As they walked back to the conference room that would be Kelsey's organization headquarters for the near future, Deke guided her with a hand on her lower back. Every time he touched her, a little thrill, like a tiny bit of electricity, shot through her veins. They hadn't been able to get together for a date since the fair on Sunday, but Deke had been texting and calling several times a day just to check in and share his day with her. When they entered the conference room, Deke closed the door behind them, took Kelsey's coffee and purse from her hands and laid them on the table. Then he wrapped his arms around her waist and pulled her close before dropping a panty-meltingly hot kiss. When Deke finally released her lips, she opened her eyes to his Cheshire Cat grin.

"Mmmmm! I have been waiting to do that since Monday, Good morning, Honey," Deke whispered in a low, sexy voice.

"Good morning to you, too, Hot Stuff!" Kelsey grinned. "Keep that up and I'm going to know you hired me just to get a little something-something at the office." She laughed.

"Now, Honey, you saw the filing system. You *know* we need your help. Kisses are just a bonus." Deke released her with a pat on her bottom. "I'm going to get out of here so you can work your magic, because if I stay, I'll only get in your way. I'll be in the office all day, so stop by and get me when you're ready for lunch."

Kelsey watched Deke's tight ass as he left the conference

room and remembered how firm the muscles felt under her fingers as he pumped into her while making love. She gave herself a little shake. Deke wasn't the only one feeling the heat between them. Her panties where already damp and all he had done was kiss her good morning. She would have to remember to pack an extra pair on the days she knew he was going to be in the office. She sighed and started in on the first box of papers.

Even though she had initially hoped to discover where Brad had gotten the money to pay for his new house, she really liked Deke and Eli and didn't feel comfortable searching through C&Y's records for the information. She made up her mind that she'd methodically work through their records and get everything in order, just as she had promised them. If she happened to stumble upon Brad's file, or, more accurately, *when* she found Brad's file, she would organize it as efficiently as she did all the other project files. Which meant she was perfectly within her job parameters to examine the paperwork. After all, when she discussed her situation with Deke at the hospital, he'd told her that he would look at the file and see if there was anything there that could help her. Since he hadn't mentioned anything, Kelsey figured there wasn't anything to find. She trusted that Deke was truly sympathetic to her situation and would help her if he could.

By lunchtime, Kelsey had worked though a couple of boxes, organizing and labeling the projects, and had started putting folders into the new filing cabinets. It had taken her a couple of hours to come up with a system that was easy enough for Deke and Eli to manage themselves, or to explain to other employees. When her stomach growled for the second time in fifteen minutes, Kelsey decided to go see if Deke was ready to make good on his offer to take her to lunch.

When she tapped on his doorframe, he looked up from what he was reading and flashed a big smile.

"Are you ever going to feed me?" she asked teasingly.

"Well, now," Deke said, with a glint in his eye, "that depends on what you're hungry for. I can promise you that I'm starving and we don't have to leave this room for me to eat what I'm craving."

Kelsey raised her eyebrows. "Is that right? Do you have a sandwich stashed in your desk that you are willing to share?"

"Why don't you shut that door and come over here and see for yourself," Deke replied and crooked his finger at her, indicating that she should come closer.

Kelsey closed the door and walked over to his desk. She didn't stop at the chair in front, but walked around the back and planted herself on his lap. She wrapped her arms around his neck and wiggled against the firm cock growing larger and larger against her hip. "Is that a sub sandwich in your pocket or are you just happy to see me?" She laughed and placed small kisses along his jaw line, making her way toward his ear.

"Oh, you are gonna pay for that," he groaned, wrapped his arms around her waist, kissed her neck, and slid a hand under the hem of her conservative black shirt. When he encountered the lacy top of her thigh-high stocking, he groaned into her neck. "Are you telling me that you have been sitting in that conference room all day wearing these sexy little stockings and I didn't know?"

Kelsey placed a small kiss on Deke's ear. "I get too hot wearing panty hose," she said simply.

Deke's hand continued up her thigh until it reached the apex. "Hmmm," Deke said as he nuzzled her neck, "these panties seem awfully damp. They must be uncomfortable. You should probably take them off."

"I should, huh? Well, I guess I wouldn't want to get chafed. Maybe you can help me take them off."

Deke rubbed her mound and she parted her thighs to give him better access. He slid a fingertip under the leg band of her panties and rubbed a tight circle around her clit. Kelsey moaned and opened her thighs wider. She reached for the edge of the desk to steady herself, and buried the other hand in the warm, silky hair at the nape of Deke's neck. She panted in an effort not to moan so loud as to draw Betty's attention from the front room.

Deke slid his fingers further into her panties and rubbed her wet slit. Suddenly, he pulled his hand away, grabbed Kelsey's waist in both hands and lifted her onto his desk. He reached under her skirt, pulled her panties down and over her strappy Mary Jayne pumps and pushed her knees apart as far as her skirt allowed. With a growl, he pulled Kelsey's bottom to the edge of the desk, pushed her skirt to her waist and buried his face in her pussy.

He parted the lips of her sex and, with his tongue, made figure eights around her little nub. Kelsey couldn't do anything but gasp for air, the pleasure was so intense. She put one hand on the top of Deke's head and held him to her as her orgasm built. When Deke plunged a finger into her pussy and sucked her clit, her orgasm washed over her like a tidal wave. She closed her thighs on his head and shuddered as wave after wave of pleasure roared through her.

Deke continued to pump his finger in her pussy, prolonging her pleasure, and lick her clit with steadily lighter and lighter pressure until she calmed enough to unlock her thighs from his head.

Kelsey loosened her grip on Deke's hair and let her thighs fall open as she tried to catch her breath. Deke nuzzled her inner thigh, pressed a kiss to the top of her bare mound and--as she lay sprawled, boneless, on top of his desk--reached to pull her to a seated position. He drew her into an embrace and held her tight until her breathing returned to normal.

As her pulse rate slowed, she realized, *Oh. My. God! I just got naked in my client's office...during working hours. What have I done?* She cringed and tried to come up with a way to handle this. *What do modern women having affairs do? I'm supposed to play it cool, right?* She wouldn't make a fuss. She would pretend this was no big deal.

When she had recovered enough to speak, she looked at Deke. He looked like a cat that had swallowed a canary. If his grin got any wider, his cheeks where going to crack. "So, that was lunch, huh? I'm not sure I will survive another meal like that." She forced a laugh..

"Honey, that was just an appetizer. The main course won't be ready until tonight." He waggled his eyebrows.

Deke was still holding her when she tensed.

"Kels, what's the matter?"

Kelsey smiled tightly and awkwardly patted his shoulder as she broke their embrace. She slid off the desk and pushed her skirt down to cover her nakedness. "Deke, I don't think I can do anything with you tonight. It's a school night and I don't usually make plans on nights when I have to get Charlie to bed early. It's too disruptive to his routine." She had turned her back to put on her panties, as modestly as possible, and brushed at her clothing.

When she turned back around, Deke stood with arms crossed, assessing her through narrowed eyes.

"What?" Kelsey asked, growing defensive. "It's not like we made plans or anything."

"What are you really saying?" he lashed out.

She stood stunned.

"So, I'm good enough to let a little steam off with, but you don't want to date me?"

Kelsey's mouth went slack. While she tried to formulate a response, she stared into his eyes and tried to rub the chill from her arms. She took a tentative step toward him and gripped his upper arms. He didn't push her away. "Deke, where is this coming from? Why in the world would you think that I don't want to date you anymore?"

He didn't answer immediately, so she continued on, "I mean, we had a great time the other night, and I thought we had fun at the fair, but you haven't actually asked me out again since then. I figured that the Single Mom thing was a little too much for you."

"Then let me be clear. I want to date you, not just sleep with you. Are you seeing someone else?" When Kelsey shook her head no, he continued, "Great, so can we get together tonight?" Deke caught her hands and rubbed his thumbs across her knuckles. "Why won't you let me in?"

Kelsey released a sigh that came from the bottom of her soul. "Deke, I just got out of a horrible marriage. Horrible! My ex-husband cheated on me. He left me for his mistress with absolutely no warning and no support. It's not like he was a lot of help before he left, but now everything in our lives is dependent upon me and the decisions I make." Kelsey pulled her hands from Deke's and turned to pace between his desk and the door.

"No matter how well I try to plan, I constantly feel like there are not enough hours in the day. I have almost every minute planned out days, if not weeks, in advance, just to keep my business and my head above water, and that all went straight to hell when I was stuck by lightening and had to take two weeks off." She got more and more agitated as she paced, staring at the ceiling and shaking her head, trying to prevent the tears that threatened to fall. "Tonight, after dinner, I have to finish a website for a client that should have been done last Friday, and Charlie has a Social Studies project that I have to help him with that is also due at the end of this week." She stopped pacing and turned toward Deke as one lone tear escaped her control. "If I drop everything tonight for you to come over, I know I will have an amazing time, but I won't have time to meet my obligations to work or my son. Please, can you understand?" she pleaded.

Deke closed his eyes and let his head fall back onto his shoulders, briefly, before looking back and crossing the room. Kelsey stood, almost vibrating with distress. He pulled her into his arms, cradled the back of her head in one big palm and gently pressed until she buried her face in neck. He sighed as she melted against him. "I'm sorry, Honey. That was *my* damage talking. Of course you have a life, and I have no right to get mad when I'm the one being inconsiderate. Will you forgive me?"

Kelsey sniffled. "Yes, but I don't understand why you would even say those things to me. I don't feel like you are only good for a roll in the sheets. I thought you knew I respected you. Why did you think I was using you like that?"

"I guess I'm not used to a woman putting sex off like that, " he said, quietly. "I've never been with a woman for more than a good time. I've been busy with my business and I didn't want to lead anyone on. I'm really no great catch, Kelsey. I guess that I am still surprised, every time I look at you, that someone as amazing as you would give me the time of day."

Kelsey raised her head from his chest and looked him in the eye. "Deacon Connelly, you are amazing. You saved my life and bring joy to my days. I am enjoying getting to know you as a person and as a lover, but I am a busy woman. I like schedules. Just because I can't always be spontaneous doesn't mean I am blowing you off."

Deke's smile was almost blinding. He kissed her softly on the lips. "How about I take you out Saturday, which is asking you out in advance, and you keep on thinking about blowing me...just not off?" he asked with a mischievous glint in his eye. Kelsey smiled back.

"Well, the first part of that is a good idea, and I will let you know how the second part plays out."

He laughed. "You've got a deal!"

CHAPTER TWENTY-THREE

Over the course of the next couple of weeks, Kelsey and Deke settled into a comfortable routine. He invited her on dates several days in advance and she did her best to take breaks from trying to organize the free world to have some fun. Deke turned out to be an adventurous and attentive boyfriend. Several times he took her out alone, but alternated those outings with activities that included Charlie. Ever since the scene on her front porch, Brad had not returned any of her phone calls and hadn't made an effort to see Charlie at all. While that left her scrambling for a babysitter every time she wanted adult time with Deke, he proved understanding if a planned outing had to be reengineered to include a six-year-old.

Deke had happily gone along with her to her Dad's sixty-fifth birthday party, where he met not only her dad, but almost all of her extended family. He happily chatted with a room full of strangers, smiled good-naturedly when Charlie spilled an entire cup of lemonade down his leg, and even managed to gracefully escape her great-aunt Edna when she demanded that he let her "feel his muscles." Her dad was already predisposed to like Deke since he'd saved Kelsey's life, but she caught her dad smiling at her and giving her a thumbs up at least three times over the course of the party. Deke definitely had her family eating out of the palm of his hand. Deke had managed to accomplish something in one afternoon that Brad had failed to accomplish in all the years that they'd been together.

The Deacon Connelly Fan Club acquired four more permanent members after Deke showed up at Della's house with a patch kit and an air pump to repair the ruptured bouncy house that was deflating to the crying wails of thirteen kids attending her son's eleventh birthday party. His hero status was further cemented when he bounced in said bouncy house with the kids at the party and didn't blink when one little partier lost all of his cake onto Deke's work boots after a somersault contest. Deke just hosed off his boots and got the kid a soda. Kelsey was definitely "in like," but The Girls were in love.

Despite the extracurricular activities, Kelsey managed to catch up at work after her forced time off. She finished the C&Y website and made huge inroads into the mess that was their filing system. She had organized and archived all of their old projects and was finally able to start on the current project boxes late Friday afternoon. She and Deke planned to meet for dinner as soon as he finished a client meeting in the showroom, so Kelsey spent the wait time scanning the contents of the five remaining boxes. "144 Spiral Drive" caught her eye. Brad's new home.

Her stomach started churning and her palms developed a sheen of moisture. The adrenaline coursing through her body made her hands shake as she lifted the lid from the seemingly innocuous brown cardboard crate. She wasn't really snooping, was she? She wasn't doing anything that she hadn't done with the rest of the boxes. This was part of the job. She had to organize this project just like all the rest. "Calm down, Kelsey, calm down, Kelsey," she repeated like a mantra. This could be nothing, but it could also be *exactly* what she and Cat needed to shed some light on how in the Great Green Goodness Brad Taggert was paying cash for a custom built luxury home.

Kelsey closed her eyes, inhaled deeply through her nose and blew the air inflating her lungs into the conference room in one huge rush. "Let's do this."

Kelsey picked up the first unlabeled file folder and shuffled through the mish-mash of papers haphazardly shoved inside. She recognized all the standard documents she'd organized in previous client files: purchase contracts...estimates... material lists...plats...and the financial guarantee. She didn't see anything different from any of the other client files. The last stack of paper shoved upside down into the file was a little larger than the rest. As Kelsey flipped it over, she spotted her bank's letterhead. She skimmed until her eye snagged on Charlie's name. Her heart stopped. She sucked in a quick breath and began reading aloud to ensure that her ears confirmed what her eyes were seeing. "This is to confirm that the funds requested, namely $1,278,000.00, are both deposited in our bank and available for withdrawal in the form of a cashier's check from the account held for the Charles Bradley Taggert Junior Trust," Kelsey read to the empty conference room, her voice getting less powerful with the shock of every word settling into her bones. The last words were barely a whisper as her heart pounded and a primal rage built in her chest.

She angrily flipped to the pages behind the bank letter in the packet to find a copy of the trust documents that the bank referenced in the letter guaranteeing payment to C&Y Construction. She read the headers of all of the paragraphs out loud.

"The Charles Bradley Taggert Junior Trust, established

blah, blah, blah," Kelsey moved through the paragraphs, and continued," The trustee of an individual child's trust shall manage and distribute the assets in the trust in the following manner: Until the trust beneficiary reaches the age specified for final distribution of the principal, the trustee may distribute some or all of the principal or net income of the trust as the trustee deems necessary for the child's health, support, maintenance and education. Education includes, but is not limited to, college, graduate, postgraduate and vocational studies and reasonable living expenses."

Kelsey dropped the pile of papers onto the conference table. Individual CHILD's trust? Oh. My. God. Brad hid the money in Charlie's name. Oh. My God. Oh. My. God. Kelsey was so angry and so astounded that she kept repeating her call to the universe.

"I have to make a copy." She pulled out her cell phone, steadied her shaking hands, and used her phone's camera function to snap two or three shots of each page, trying to up the odds that at least one of them would be legible. It was almost impossible to keep the device steady when all of the blood in her body had been replaced by burning hot lava.

Fourteen pages and about eighty-seven pictures later, Kelsey dropped her cell phone onto the conference table next to the basket of vipers shaped like a contract. God, her head ached. How had this happened? What was she going to do? Why hadn't Deke shown this to her before now? He had to have known about it...he was the one, after all, who had told her that Brad was paying cash. Why would he have kept this from her? Was he afraid she would stop the build and cost him a bunch of money? Was he trying to cover his tracks because he knew that he and Eli were doing something wrong? Oh, my God, was he keeping this from her until he was done screwing her and THEN tell her? Was she just some piece of ass to him? Oh, God! How could she have been so stupid? Deke must have been laughing about how easy it was to get her into bed...poor old Kelsey Taggert. Couldn't keep her husband, but maybe she would be grateful if he paid her a little attention. What a fool....

She pressed her fingers against her eyes, trying to stop the pounding behind her eye sockets. As she tried to rub the images of the contracts from her eyes, the conference room door opened.

"Hey, Pretty Lady! Ready for a break?"

Kelsey slowly lifted her head as her hands dropped lifelessly onto the conference table. She looked directly into Deke's compelling gaze and her anger and despair spiked.

“You knew!" she spat at him.

“Knew what?" Deke's brow crinkled with confusion.

“You knew that Brad hid money in Charlie's name! How could you lie to me?" Kelsey demanded. "It's all right here." She smacked the stack of papers in front of her with open palms. Deke's face flashed from confused to blank to indignant in the course of seconds. "Now wait just one minute," he declared, "I don't know what you are talking about, but I have never lied to you....never!"

Kelsey angrily shoved the small stack of papers in Deke's direction and crossed her arms. "You might want to rethink that 'never,' pal. I found the documents for my ex's house. You knew! You knew all along that he had a trust in Charlie's name!"

Deke picked up the stack of papers, took a quick look and dropped it back on the table, raising his eyes to meet Kelsey's stony gaze.

"Why did you bother to lie to me?" Kelsey demanded. "You had to know that I would find these papers when I organized the office. I guess you just figured that you would get into my bed while the getting was good, huh? " She shook her head and harrumphed. "Well, you thought wrong, Asshole."

"Now wait just one minute, Kelsey! I did NOT know anything about this paperwork. That is Eli's department! I concentrate on the plans and the project. Eli runs the office end of things..*INCLUDING THE MONEY!*"

Kelsey sat, arms crossed tightly across her chest, slowly shaking her head. She looked Deke in the eye and would have sworn that he was telling the truth, but the proof lay in front of her. Of COURSE she had read him wrong. She had read her ex-husband wrong *FOR YEARS*. She was an easy mark. A pushover. Everyone said so.. "I should have known better," she whispered. "I should have known you were too good to be true." A tear rolled down her cheek, but she was too busy trying to hold herself together to lift her hand and wipe it away.

Deke circled the conference table and tried to put his arms around Kelsey, but she raised her hands and pushed his arms away. He lifted his hands, palms out, to show he got her message that she didn't want to be touched, but he continued to plead his case. "Please, Kelsey, don't cry. This is a mistake. We will figure this out."

Kelsey finally lifted her arm, palm out, crying, "Stop, just...stop!" Deke's advance faltered and Kelsey got up and moved around the end of the conference table toward the door. "I can't do this," her voice cracked and she barely kept the tears at bay. "I can't trust you. You knew this and you didn't tell me. I..I just...I have to go." Kelsey grabbed her purse from the chair next to the door and stopped at the front door only long enough to grab her coat and head out the front door. She heard Deke's voice calling out, but she was already across the street and pulling open her car door. As she pulled out into traffic, she saw Deke, standing on the front steps of the remodeled front porch, arms hanging by his side, watching her drive away.

CHAPTER TWENTY-FOUR

Deke watched Kelsey's car until she turned at the corner and drove beyond his sight. He lifted his right hand to rub his sternum to try to alleviate the burning sensation that had been building since Kelsey backed away from him in the conference room. From the start, he had known she was damaged. He knew that Brad had treated her like shit and that she had this tough shell, but he had believed that, if he went slow enough, and treated her like a woman *should* be treated, that she would let him in. He had to admit defeat. His arm dropped to his sides and he stared at the street corner where Kelsey's taillights had disappeared.

Hearing Kelsey accuse him of lying was one thing, but the look of absolute conviction on her face when she accused him of using her was damning. She believed it. She had no faith in him at all. All of his efforts had been for nothing. Deke's sigh was so long and deep that he almost felt dizzy. Kelsey Taggert would never love him. He turned, walked up the steps, opened the door to the office and went to tell Eli what had just happened.

CHAPTER TWENTY-FIVE

Two nights later, Kelsey sat in a local Mexican restaurant with The Girls, celebrating finding the proof she needed to bring her ex husband to his knees. "To Best Friends," Kelsey called out, raising her half-empty Cosmo to the ladies surrounding her at the sticky bar table.

"Here, Here!" called her favorite ladies in the entire world. After everyone took a sip of their respective cocktails, Kelsey felt a hand wrap itself warmly around the one that was not clutching her drink.

"For someone who just found the wooden stake to end the reign of the emotional vampire you call an ex-husband, you sure don't look happy, Kelsey. What gives?" asked Cat.

Kelsey looked down at the table and fidgeted with the damp cocktail napkin under the long stemmed martini glass in front of her. "I think I did something really stupid."

"Well, what was it? Maybe we can help," Lyssie chirped. She was a fixer so a good strategy session was right up her alley.

“Uh...." She faltered. "Well...I *might* have accused Deke of hiding the trust documents from me so he could get into my ..." Kelsey's voice petered out as the rest of her friends uttered gasps or almost choked on sharp intakes of breath. All she heard was a collective "What?" that sounded like it a shout through a megaphone.

"Don't start on me, okay?" Kelsey begged, tearing up and raising her voice to be heard over Cat's moaning and Lyssie's tsking and even Jayne's "mmm, mmm, mmm" and head shaking. The only person not taking her to task was Della.

Della stared with her forehead all scrunched up and her eyebrows bunched as if Kelsey had just started spouting Portuguese Pirate Shanties. "What in the wide world of sports would have made you do something *that boneheaded?"*

"Well, thanks for all of your support!" Kelsey snarked.

"Come on, Kelsey...you don't actually believe that crap do you?" Cat asked. "The man is in love with you! Every single one of us knows that!"

Kelsey raised her wide eyes to Cat's gaze and saw the truth in her friend's face. As her gaze traveled from Cat's face to meet the eyes of the rest of her friends around the table, she saw nothing but matching looks of sincerity and confidence. "You think..." Kelsey stumbled and then continued, "you ALL think that Deacon Connelly is in *love?* With ME?" She must have looked as incredulous as she felt, because Cat snorted and the rest of the girls started laughing. Laughing hysterically at *her.* Are you kidding me here? Have I entered a parallel universe or something?

Lyssie calmed down enough to answer, but was still giggling as she declared, "Of COURSE he is in love with you, Dumb Ass! He washed your car for you! He threatened to beat up your ex-husband, who happens, by the way, to be a CLIENT of HIS! Hell, he passed through all of our hazing with flying colors. Jesus, Kelsey! Della's kid puked on his shoes and he just laughed and made Charlie a balloon animal. If that's not true love, I don't know WHAT is!"

Kelsey couldn't laugh. She just sat, with her mouth slightly open, with the same thought on a loop, running through her mind. "Oh my god. Oh my god. He loves me. What have I done?"

Jayne reached over and took Kelsey's hand. "Look, Kelsey. I am sure you are making it out to be worse than it is, Just call him!"

“Yeah, what's his number?" Cat demanded, snatching Kelsey's cell phone from the outside pocket of the purse hanging on the back of her chair. "I'll call him right now."

Kelsey snatched her phone back and scooted her chair from the table. "No, I'll call him." She moved her finger down the frequently called list and touched the telephone icon to ring Deke as she maneuvered her way through the crowded restaurant bar and out into the cool evening air on the almost abandoned patio. His phone rang four times and went to voicemail.

"Hey, Deke. It's Kelsey. Listen, I really need to talk to you. I think I owe you an apology. Please call me back when you get this. Thanks." Kelsey pushed the red "end call" button, turned, reentered the bar and rejoined her friends.

"I just got his voicemail." Kelsey sighed, sitting back down and pulling her lukewarm cocktail toward her as she set her phone on the table next to her.

"I'm sure he will call soon," Jayne said, patting Kelsey's hand.

Kelsey nodded and smiled, but, in her heart, she wasn't so sure. As she tried to finish her drink, she flashed back to the devastated look on Deke's face, glimpsed in her rearview mirror as she drove away. It was going to take more than a few phone calls to get through to Deke. It is going to take some real effort to get him to forgive her for jumping to such a terrible conclusion. As soon as this court thing was over, she would devote all of her time to winning Deke back. First, though, she owed it to Charlie, and *herself*, to make sure that Brad paid for what he had tried to do to their son.

CHAPTER TWENTY-SIX

Kelsey sat in the empty courtroom at the Plaintiff's table with her hands tightly folded, gripping her fingers until her knuckles whitened. Theirs was the first hearing of the morning, so, for the time being, they had the courtroom to themselves. Cat sat next to her, reviewing files to make sure she had all of the details ready to present the most concise case possible. Cat looked up from her notes and must have seen Kelsey's agitation. Cat placed her hands over Kelsey's tightly clenched ones.

"It's going to be fine, Kelsey, so just relax. We have all of the facts on our side. There is no way the judge is not going to find in our favor." Cat had dressed for battle in a killer black suit and sky-high stilettos. She called this her "Man Eater" look and she was ready to make Brad's legal counsel bleed.

With the information the forensic accountant dug up after Kelsey found the copy of the "C.B. Taggert Trust" check in Brad's building file, Cat assured her they had a slam dunk case against Brad for fraud. Her killer attorney friend was going to ask the judge to turn all of the remaining assets in the trust over to Kelsey and to put Kelsey's name on the deed to the home Brad had built so that half of it would belong to her. If Brad didn't want Kelsey's name on the deed, then he would have to find a way to buy her out of her half at fair market value. The next call Cat said she was going to make would be to the IRS, but *that* was just for fun.

Brad and his legal counsel strolled into the courtroom minutes before the start of the hearing, so Kelsey was spared the necessity of making small talk with her small-minded ex. Brad's attorney opened his briefcase and began to set up his notes at the Respondent's designated table across the aisle. Cat slowly rose from her seat and sashayed over to drop a copy of the cancelled check to C&Y Construction on the table in front of Brad's lawyer.

"What's this?" asked the attorney, with a confused pucker to his brow.

Cat stared at him with a look that would make any man cringe. "That's what we will be asking your client to explain to the judge. It seems that Mr. C.B. Taggert, here, wasn't completely forthcoming with his financial disclosure during the original divorce proceedings." Cat smirked and waited for the other lawyer to respond.

"I thought we were here to go over some inconsistencies with their joint tax returns," he sputtered. "I don't know anything about any trust!" The visibly uncomfortable attorney turned to Brad and asked, "What is this?"

Brad just looked at him with a bored expression. "That is something that was not part of our joint assets. I set up a trust in my son's name. I am the trustee and it is all legal and above-board. The Nevada attorney said there is no way that Kelsey can touch any of it, because it's legally in the kid's name, so I don't have to tell her anything about it."

Cat and Brad's attorney looked at him like he had lost his

mind. Cat turned to opposing counsel and said, "Oh, I'm going to enjoy this!"

The court reporter and the Bailiff entered the courtroom as Cat returned to her table and took her seat next to Kelsey.

"All rise!" called the Bailiff, "the Honorable Gregory Barrett presiding." As the darkly robed man serving as judge for the hearing came out the hallway leading from his chambers, everyone stood. As the judge took his seat, he looked up at everyone with a harried expression, quickly stating, "Be seated."

Kelsey was so nervous that she couldn't look anywhere but straight ahead. Everything hinged on today's outcome. As soon as this was over and she had secured Charlie's future, she could concentrate on finding a way to get Deke to forgive her.

The judge looked up from his docket and said, "Good morning, Ladies and Gentlemen. It looks like we are here to re-examine a disbursement of marital assets in the Dissolution of Marriage between Charles Bradley Taggert and Kelsey Ann Taggert. Are both parties present?"

Cat stood up and answered, "Yes, Your Honor. Catherine Marston for the Plaintiff."

Brad's counsel stood and replied, "Yes, Your Honor. Eric Peters for the Respondent."

"Very good," Judge Barrett said. "Now, as you both know, it is very unusual to reopen a property settlement in a dissolution case, so I trust there is a very serious reason for your request."

"Yes, Your Honor," Cat replied. "We are asking that you revisit the matter of Mr. Taggert's disclosure, or rather lack thereof, during the previous proceedings, surrounding a trust worth more than one million dollars."

The judge's brow puckered and he raised his eyebrows. "That is a significant amount of money, Counsel," Judge

Barrett said. "Mr. Peters, what does your client have to say about the matter?"

Brad's attorney fidgeted. "Your Honor, I just found out about the matter a few moments ago. Could I have a few minutes to confer with my client?"

"I think I would rather hear directly from the Respondent. Mr. Taggert, what is the C.B. Taggert Trust?"

Brad looked at the judge and said, "It is a trust that I set up for my son, Charles, Your Honor. The funds legally belong to him and I was assured by my attorney that the trust would not be part of my divorce settlement."

Judge Barrett looked perplexed. "Mr. Peters, I'm confused. Didn't you serve as Mr. Taggert's legal counsel during his Dissolution last year? You are listed in the court documents as the attorney of record."

"Yes, I did, Your Honor, but I am not the attorney that advised Mr. Taggert about this trust."

The judge looked at Brad. "Mr. Taggert, care to explain?"

"I used a lawyer in Vegas. That's where I won the money," Brad said, apparently annoyed with the entire process.

Cat looked at Kelsey questioningly, but Kelsey didn't understand either. Then, a memory bubbled up. Hadn't Barbie told everyone at Charlie's birthday party last year that she met Brad in Las Vegas? Kelsey had imbibed a lot of tequila, trying not to stab her ex for showing up unannounced at her kid's birthday party dragging his stripper girlfriend, but she was sure she had gotten that one detail correct, even if most of the party was fuzzy.

Kelsey grabbed Cat's legal pad and pen and wrote, "Brad met Boobs in Vegas!"

Cat raised her eyebrows and then got a predatory gleam in her eye. "Your Honor, can Mr. Taggert please tell the court exactly *when* he won the money he used to fund the trust for his son?"

The judge looked at Brad. "Mr. Taggert?"

"I was in Las Vegas for my company's sales recognition trip. It was last April. I won the trip for selling the most Cadillacs in the first quarter." Brad preened. "One night, I was out at one of the casinos waiting to have dinner with some of the other winners from Cadillac when I stuck a couple of bucks into one of those giant slot machines next to the Hostess stand and I won! The jackpot was two point five million bucks and I won!" Brad's story might have been compelling if everyone in the room wasn't so disgusted with his attitude.

Kelsey couldn't believe her ears! After all of those years supporting him and his stupid theater career, the asshole had won two and a half million bucks and didn't tell her about it. It suddenly became clear that she had been married to one of the lowest human beings on the face of the earth.

Cat interjected, "Your Honor, we would like to raise the issue that Mr. Taggert did not serve Mrs. Taggert with a Notice of Divorce until June of last year, a full two months after he says he won this money, but nothing at all was mentioned in the financial disclosure documents."

Brad piped up, "Well, the lawyer that the casino found for me said he could structure the trust so I wouldn't have to give my wife any of the money in the event we divorced, so I didn't think I had to tell Kelsey anything about it."

The judge waited a full minute after Brad had stopped speaking and then said, in a slow, even tone, "Now, let me get this straight. You won a slot machine jackpot to the tune of more than two million dollars while you were married to Mrs. Taggert, but you didn't tell her about it, correct?"

"Well, yeah, but..." Brad started, but Judge Barrett raised a hand to stop Brad from speaking.

"Then you followed the advice of a lawyer in Nevada who told you that, if you put the money into a trust in your son's name, that you could keep your wife from getting any of the money if you decided to divorce. Is that about right?" Judge Barrett asked.

"Yes," Brad confirmed.

"Mr. Taggert, you disgust me. I see the worst of human behavior in my courtroom, but this is certainly one for the record books. First off, let me start by telling you that I am going to thoroughly enjoy delivering the following information to you. It gives me great pleasure to tell you that the legal advice you received in Nevada has absolutely nothing to do with the law pertaining to marital assets in the Commonwealth of Kentucky. The moment you won the jackpot, the funds belonged equally to you *and* Mrs. Taggert as your wife. You had no right under the law to hide those assets from her. I am ordering a full accounting of all of the funds that were deposited in the trust and I am awarding one half of the original amount of money be paid to Mrs. Taggert as an equitable distribution of the marital estate," the judge declared.

Kelsey gasped and Brad jumped up and yelled, "Now, wait a minute! You can't do that! Most of it has been spent on a house I'm building for my fiancée!" His attorney put a hand on Brad's arm to calm him down and the judge banged his gavel.

"Mr. Taggert, control yourself or I will have the bailiff remove you!" Judge Barrett waited for Brad to sit back down and then continued with his ruling. "I also see here, in the court's history of child support payments, that you have not made a scheduled child support payment through the court managed payment system since ...and correct me if I'm wrong... this week NINE MONTHS AGO." Judge Barrett looked at Brad, as if waiting for Brad to comment, but since the Brastard did nothing but sputter, Judge Barrett continued. "So, you lied about your assets and you don't pay child support. Does that about sum it up, Counsel?"

Brad's attorney muttered, "Apparently so, Your Honor."

"Uh-huh!" Judge Barrett harrumphed. "Well, Mr. Taggert, since you admit that you acquired funds during the period of your marriage and you colluded with outside counsel to purposefully hide these assets from your wife in anticipation of divorcing her, the law also allows me to award her damages. I am awarding Kelsey Anne Taggert the remaining fifty percent of the trust assets as damages for the fraud you committed against her and this court. I will leave it up to legal counsel to collect the appropriate documentation, but I am giving you one week to provide an exact accounting of all of the funds from the C.B. Taggert Trust and to deliver the proceeds of the trust and any assets that have been purchased with those funds to Mrs. Kelsey Anne Taggert's custody. You, Mr. Taggert, are a deadbeat. This court despises deadbeats. I hope you have learned your lesson. Court adjourned!"

Brad kept staring at the judge's bench with his mouth hanging slightly open. Kelsey knew he was in shock, but she didn't feel the slightest remorse for his pain. Kelsey couldn't believe what a selfish monster Brad had turned out to be. She had never given him much credit as a husband, but she would never have believed that he would hide all of that money from her without even a second thought. She hoped he enjoyed struggling, like she had done, without all of his cash. She wondered just how long his so-called fiancée would stick around once she found out that Brad was broke.

As the judge reached the door leading to his chambers, Brad jumped out of his chair and started sputtering, "Wait! You can't do that! Hey! Come back here!" When Brad started around the table like he was going to follow the judge back to his chambers, the Bailiff who had been holding the door for Judge Barrett headed toward Brad to cut him off. Brad's attorney jumped up and laid a restraining arm across his client's chest, demanding that Brad calm down. Brad turned his furious gaze on his attorney.

"How could you let this happen?" he demanded. "We have to appeal! What the hell am I paying you for?" Brad railed on and on about how this was no one's business but his, and how could his attorney be so incompetent, while waving his finger in Eric Peters' face and threatening to have him disbarred.

Eric's face turned to granite as he faced off against his angry client. "I will remind you, Mr. Taggert," Eric intoned with a voice so cold that even Kelsey got goose bumps, "that you agreed to have a fast-track divorce, with a binding mediation in place of a hearing, so that you could, and I quote, 'Upgrade to Wife 2.0.' There IS no appeal here and, even if there was, you would have to find new counsel. You disgust me, and if you don't get that scrawny little finger out of my face, I am going to snap it off and mail it back to you with my final bill!" Eric Peters slammed his briefcase closed, sent a sympathetic look toward Cat and turned his back on the fuming client that he had just fired.

Brad yelled at the Bailiff, "He just THREATENED ME! Arrest him! You heard him!"

The Bailiff calmly returned Brad's stare and simply stated, "I didn't hear anything back here. Do you need me to assist you to the elevator?"

"Oh my god! You people are going to pay for this! All of you!" Brad stomped toward the courtroom exit and tried to pull the door open to leave. His dramatic exit was derailed when he pulled three times, grunting as if he were moving boulders, but the door still wouldn't open.

The Bailiff strolled over to where Brad struggled, calling the door names, calmly raised his arm, and pushed the door open. "Here you go. Have a nice day now." Brad growled and stomped through the door, the bailiff shaking his head like this was just another day full of idiots in his courtroom.

While all of this went on, Kelsey sat in her chair, her eyes wide and mouth slightly open, too stunned to move. She was even too stunned to laugh at Brad trying to pull his way through a door that everyone had to push to open.

She had won!

She looked over at Cat and then grabbed her friend in a tight embrace. "We did it! We did it!" Kelsey held on to Cat and kept repeating the phrase. After a few minutes, Cat gently nudged her to release the embrace. Only then did Kelsey notice Brad's attorney hovering near their table.

"I'll have the paperwork to you as soon as I can. I expect to have to get a court order from the judge ordering the bank to release the trust records, since I don't expect Mr. Taggert to make this easy." He gave a tight smile and said, "I'll be in touch."

After Mr. Peters walked away, Cat turned to Kelsey and said, "Let's go celebrate, Money Bags! Lunch is on you!"

CHAPTER TWENTY-SEVEN

Kelsey fussed with her outfit as she waited in the boardroom of the title company. Today was the day that she signed the final sales paperwork for the house that Brad and Barbie had commissioned from C&Y Construction. Even though she was awarded the house because of the judge's ruling, the construction company still held title, technically, because Brad hadn't closed on the property before the ruling was handed down. She knew that she and Charlie would never be happy there, so she had the house listed as soon as the court paperwork was finalized.

The real estate agent that Kelsey consulted had advised that a finished house would sell better in that market, so Kelsey had arranged with Eli and his team to finish up so the house could be listed as ready to move into. She wanted the best price the market would bear; not because she wanted to turn a profit, but because she wanted to provide as much security for Charlie's future as possible. Even after the judge had awarded all of the money to Kelsey, it didn't feel right to her to take it for herself. It made her feel dirty to even think about it. Instead, she had asked the judge if he would agree to keep the trust in Charlie's name and make her the Trustee until his twenty-fifth birthday. Judge Barrett had agreed and the bank was more than happy to help with the paperwork if she kept the money in their care.

It had been more than a month since she had stormed out of Deke's office, and she had not seen or talked to him once. When she got the stunning news of her legal victory, the first person she had wanted to call was Deke, but when she called, he didn't pick up the phone. She really missed him, but she was so busy trying to tie up all of the loose ends to finalize the house sale that she hadn't had time to formulate a solid plan of how to approach him. Brad hadn't asked to see Charlie a single time since his underhanded dealings had been brought to light, and trying to be both father and mother to her son left her with even less time than she had had before.

The days blurred together, but the ache in her heart where Deke used to be never dulled. She had no idea where the last few weeks had gone or how she was going to find happiness when her heart lacked a vital piece. She only knew that, when she laid down to sleep at night, all she dreamed about was a tall, black haired man staring at her with sad green eyes, always out of reach, no matter how fast she ran or how she pleaded for him to come back. She had run miles and miles in her dreams.

The Girls had tried to coax her into going out on the town with them to celebrate the court decision, but Kelsey invented excuses to stay home. She knew they were going to nag her to come up with a plan to get Deke back, but she just couldn't talk to them about it anymore. Her feelings were too raw for a cheerleading session to fix, even if the cheerleaders were her best friends in the entire world. It just hurt too much.

It was all she could do to keep up a brave front when Charlie asked about Deke. She kept assuring him that Deke was busy, but she hoped he would be back soon. She hoped... because she couldn't bear the alternative. She was almost out of time. She doubted that Deke would agree to meet her, but she was hoping that if she kept frequenting every place she had ever remembered him saying he liked, that she could "run into him by accident" and beg him give her a chance to apologize. She visited the coffee shop where they had met at least three times a week, eaten at the pizza place that he claimed was his favorite for lunch enough times that she was becoming a "regular," stopped by the hardware store on her way to dropping Charlie at school to look at the Contractor line, and even made the trek out to his mom's café, hoping to catch him. She had not caught even a glimpse of Deke in four weeks. A this point, she was going to have to enlist outside help to get him into the same room with her. Her last hope was Eli.

Kelsey had avoided bringing up her relationship with Deke to Eli during their meetings about the house because it wasn't right to put him in the middle between his friend and his client. Now that the house was finished, Kelsey was desperate enough to overcome any qualms she might have about Eli's feelings. She loved Deke and, even if he never wanted to see her again, she HAD to apologize. Today was the day that she put the screws to Eli.

The buyer's real estate agent had the final paperwork signed and ready for C&Y Construction to release the property to Charlie's trust and transfer title to the new homeowners. She expected Eli to arrive any minute with the title company representative. She watched ducks paddling about a pond outside the room's picture window while she rehearsed the speech she would give Eli in an attempt to secure his assistance. Voices outside the conference room door snapped her back to the present. The door opened behind her. She turned with a smile to greet the arrivals but her smile froze and then faded in shock when Deke trailed the title agency's representative through the door.

Deke turned his head and their eyes locked. He abruptly stopped talking, but moved his eyes away from Kelsey's gaze and looked out the window, not even saying hello. Jake, the clerk from the title agency, still talking, placed his folder of documents onto the table, not noticing that Deke had stopped responding. He smiled at Kelsey and said, "Okay, Ms. Taggert, since Mr. Connelly from C&Y is here now, we can get things moving."

When Kelsey didn't respond, he gestured to the table in front of her where he had placed a pile of paperwork without her notice.

Kelsey gripped the straps of the purse in her lap to keep them from shaking. She focused on the paperwork, trying to recover from the shock of Deke refusing to acknowledge her in any way. He wouldn't even look at her! She didn't register that Jake was talking to her, she was so lost in the man who had been haunting her dreams. His hair was a little longer and he hadn't shaved in a while, but he was just as handsome as ever. Deke stopped staring out of the window, but he still refused to meet her eyes.

"Ms. Taggert? Kelsey? Is everything all right?" Jake asked. His concerned tone finally broke through her haze.

She looked quickly at Jake, but returned to her perusal of Deke, saying, "Sorry, yes, I'm fine. Let's get started."

As Jake started to pass papers to her, indicating she should sign next to the little stickers, Kelsey was grateful for the little red "sign here" adhesive arrows, or she would have been at a total loss as to what she was supposed to be doing. The motion of signing her name over and over again gave Kelsey a few minutes to regain her composure and return her breathing to normal. When she signed the last page, she passed the pile of documents back to Jake.

"Now, Deke, if you could sign under Ms. Taggert's signature on all of these, we will be done here," Jake said. Deke started signing his name on the pages indicated. When he finished, he passed the messy stack back to Jake. The title clerk tapped the documents into a neat pile and said, "Okay, that's it! These are ready to go to the buyers. Thank you both for your time. Once everything has been properly filed with the County Clerk's office, we will mail your certified copies to you. Let me show you out." Deke held out his hand to shake with Jake, gave the man a tight smile, and turned on his heel to leave the conference room, all without looking at Kelsey.

Kelsey didn't bother to return Jake's niceties as she grabbed her purse and ran around the conference table and out the door. She didn't know what she was going to say when she caught up with him, but she knew this might be her final chance to see him again. His strides were so long, he had already made it to the lobby door and was pushing it open when she came around the corner.

"Deke! Wait!" Kelsey called, but he either ignored her or didn't hear her because he was already out the door. She hurried across the lobby and pushed through the door. He was halfway across the parking lot. She meant to call out in a louder voice as she started down the steps, but she lost her footing and yelped as she tumbled down the concrete steps and landed hard on hands and knees on the sidewalk below. She knelt there, dazed for a moment before the pain from her scrapes and a twisted ankle hit her. She sat down on her bottom and burst into hysterical sobs, burying her face in her scraped and bloody hands.

She didn't hear anyone approach. But suddenly she was lifted onto the lap of someone smelling like lumber and citrus. She looked up into a pair of startlingly green eyes.

He pushed hair off her face and cupped her cheek briefly, wiping away her tears. He smiled briefly, but his eyes were almost impassive, like he was looking at a stranger. His touch was impersonal as moved his hands down her arms and legs searching for injuries. When he reached her ankle, he stopped. It was already swelling.

"Honey, you have *got* to stop falling down to get my attention."

Kelsey was so relieved to hear the familiar endearment that she cried harder. She buried her face in the front of his shirt and sobbed her heart out.

Deke hugged her gently and said, "Kelsey, I'm sorry! I know you're hurt. I shouldn't joke. I was just trying to lighten the mood a little. I didn't mean to make fun of you. Kelsey, please don't cry. Do you want to go to the hospital for that ankle? I know it hurts. It's probably sprained, but it might be broken. Come on, Kels, talk to me!"

She continued to sob because her heart hurt so much more than her ankle. The look in Deke's eyes had said it all. It was too late. He felt nothing for her now. She had ruined it all.

Suddenly, Kelsey realized just how pathetic she must seem. She needed to get away from here. She couldn't stand for him to see her like this. She pushed away from Deke's chest and tried to climb out of his lap. He tightened his hold to keep her from wriggling away. "Stop it! You're going to hurt yourself more. Let me help you," he hissed.

"Please let me go," Kelsey said, trying to control her crying. "I'm fine. Just let me get up."

"Kelsey, you are *not* fine. You're bleeding and your ankle is swollen, now let me help you," Deke said.

"No," she said, as firmly and calmly as she could. "Just go on. I'll take care of myself." She sniffled. "Please, let me up. *Please.*" Her voice broke on the last word and the little bit of pride she had left fled when she pushed with the last of her strength and couldn't shift Deke's arms.

All of the fight left her and she collapsed into a boneless heap in his lap. Tears ran in continuous rivulets down her cheeks, but she didn't say anything. She was too tired to move. The month away from Deke had been hard, but she kept holding out hope that she could explain it all to him and he would understand. Now, seeing how distant he was, even while she was as close as she could be to him physically, she finally realized that she had been a fool, believing that everything would be fine once she explained it all to him. He looked at her like she was a stranger. It was over. Deke wasn't interested in any explanation. He was done. If he had shown even a spark of emotion, she would have thrown herself at his feet and begged his forgiveness. This dispassionate man in front of her didn't want to hear her excuses. She wouldn't make either one of them any more uncomfortable than they already were. She had spent years being the only person in her marriage willing to work to keep it together and even her best had not been enough. Clearly, Deke was not as much in love as she was. It was over.

A sense of calm washed over her. There was something freeing about letting go, even when it was heartbreakingly sad. Even her divorce from Brad hadn't been this devastating, because she had not been in love with him anymore.

She knew, at that moment, that Deacon Connelly was the first man in her life that she had ever truly loved. Funny that she would figure that out at the moment when she also learned that she had lost him forever. The old Kelsey would have broken into a million pieces, but the new Kelsey had been forged in fire...in *lightning*, even.

New Kelsey's heart had scars that hurt now because they were new and tight, but that heart would be stronger for loving Deke. She still had that good life she'd built for herself and her son after Brad left. Even if her bed was a little colder, she knew she could go on, even if it meant moving on without Deke Connelly.

Kelsey got her breathing under control and once again, in the calmest voice she could muster, said, "Deke, please let me go. If you can just help me stand, I'm sure I can take it from there." The change in her demeanor must have convinced him that she was okay because he loosened his hold. She wiped her eyes and stared at a button on Deke's shirt before she began to shift her legs in anticipation of rising.

Deke's hold tightened as she shifted in preparation to stand, as though the manners ingrained in him since childhood wouldn't allow him to see a woman struggle on her own if he could help. She picked up her purse from the sidewalk, looped the strap across her body and started to put weight onto her uninjured foot, using Deke's forearm and then his shoulder to steady herself. Once she stood upright, she gingerly shifted weight onto her sore ankle and found it painful but able to bear some weight. Assured that it was twisted and not more seriously injured, Kelsey released Deke's forearm, where she had been holding on for balance.

She tried to smile at him, but was sure it looked like a grimace. It took all of her remaining control to keep her lip from trembling. "See, it looks worse than it is. I'll be fine. Thank you, again, for stopping to help." She gave a short laugh. "I promise this will be the last time I fall in front of you. Good luck, Deke. Please tell Eli the same." She tried to smile, but had to turn away, afraid she was going to start crying all over again. She took her first tentative step toward her car when Deke's voice stopped her.

"Kelsey," he whispered in a pained tone, "wait."

She turned back and saw raw pain in his eyes. She stood there, unsure what to do. Hadn't he just ignored her when she called out to him to try to explain? Hadn't she humiliated herself enough for one day? What more did he want from her? Her heart couldn't take this up and down ride. She didn't have any fight left. So she stood, frozen in time, waiting for him to speak.

"I—" Deke started and then stopped. He shoved a hand through his unkempt hair and blew a long breath. Then he started again. "I miss you."

Kelsey didn't know what to say or do.

"Aren't you going to say anything?" Deke asked.

"What do you want me to say?" Kelsey asked in a small, pained voice. "Do you want me to tell you that I miss you? Because I have...almost every moment we have been apart. Do you want me to tell you that I'm sorry? Because I tried that, but you wouldn't return my phone calls and you didn't return any of my messages. Do you want me to throw myself at your feet and tell you that I love you? Because I do love you, with all of my heart, but it's not enough...and I have *definitely* been on the ground enough lately," she said with a short, humorless laugh.

"You love me? Did you just say that you *love me?*" Deke asked incredulously.

"Uh, yeah..." Kelsey didn't finish before he stood, picked her up and kissed her within an inch of her life. Deke's arms crushed her to his chest. She open her lips and his tongue invaded her mouth. When he finally let her up for air, they were both breathing so hard that neither could speak.

Kelsey stared at him and finally asked, "Why did you do that?"

"Because, you infuriating woman, I love you!" He laughed and pressed tiny kisses to her face. Kelsey closed her eyes and nuzzled his whiskered jaw. She could not believe that he held her, when moments ago, she was sure she would never see him again.

"You *love me?*" she asked, still not believing that she had heard him correctly.

"God help me, I do." Deke lifted his head and met her confused gaze. "You almost ripped the heart right out of my chest when you accused me of lying to you. I would *never* do something like that, Kelsey, even if I didn't love you like I do. I am not that kind of man. I may not be the sharpest knife in the drawer, but I would never help someone commit fraud, especially against their own kid and *never* against someone I care about."

"My heart knew that even when my mind was making my mouth say those awful things to you." Kelsey placing her hand on his furry cheek. "I was just so upset, and I lashed out without thinking. I knew you would never do that, but I let my emotions take control of my mouth and just blew up. I regretted it as soon as I said it, but I was in my car before I even realized I had left. I called so many times to apologize and you wouldn't take any of my calls or return my messages."

"I know. I'm sorry about that. I have never been in love before. I couldn't believe how much it hurt to hear you say those things about me. I figured that you wouldn't have believed that I could have done something like that, even for a minute, if you had any real feelings for me. I was too hurt to see things from your perspective. None of that seemed important anymore, though, when I saw you in that conference room."

"What are you talking about?" Kelsey asked. "You wouldn't even *look* at me!".

"I couldn't, Honey. I was afraid I was going to drop down to my knees right there on the floor and beg you to come back to me. I had almost no pride left, and it took all I could muster to sign those papers and get the hell out without making a total fool of myself."

Kelsey stared adoringly into the eyes of the man she

loved. "I would have appreciated someone *else* doing the falling for a change," she said, eyes twinkling.

Deke threw his head back and laughed. "I promise I will do all of the falling from now on."

Kelsey believed him...except for the falling in love....they were going to do that *together*.

WHAT HAPPENS NEXT?

Look for Lucky Streak, Book 2 in the Lucky, Kentucky Saga coming soon! Read an excerpt below then sign up for Cate Beaumont's newsletter at www.catebeaumont.com/newsletter to be alerted when it's released.

Chapter 1

Catherine Marston sighed so deeply that she almost became lightheaded. She was sitting in a club sipping a cocktail that she didn't even want and listening to the most obnoxious pop music that she had heard in her entire life. She waffled between being grateful that her two brothers had been fans of speed metal and being petulant about the fact that she had lost another bet to her best friend Della and had been forced to make good on her "Della's choice Night Out" marker on a night when none of their other friends were able to join in the fun. Bitches.

Man, Cat hated strip clubs. In fact, hatred was not a strong enough word for how Cat felt about strip clubs. Detested was close. Abhorred was better. She hated them so much that she had to be tricked into attending her own bachelorette party. The fact that she had no use for strip clubs was a well-known fact that she had reinforced on many occasions when her friends had attempted to coerce her into attending parties for engaged friends trying to celebrate their impending nuptials or recently divorced friends celebrating their newly inked and filed freedom from the old ball and chain. The repugnance that Cat felt for strip clubs was so absolute and so widely known among her group of friends and acquaintances that it was absolutely astounding to her that she was sitting in one right that moment.

No matter how upscale Club Jester was reputed to be, it was still a bar where a group of nearly naked, oiled up men would be shaking their steroid swollen bodies for a bunch of hormonally challenged women in the hopes of separating the ladies and their cash any minute now. Della really knew how to exact the most revenge possible out of each and every one of the ladies that made up their group of best friends, The Girls.

Cat perched carefully on the smooth leather bar stool, trying her best to ignore her smirking blond friend seated next to her, humming along to the latest Top 40 tunes being blasted over the sound system as the bar's patrons waited for the live entertainment to begin. Of course, Della had reserved a table right in front of the stage to ensure that Cat's punishment was as complete as possible. The raised platform in front of them featured several metal poles fastened firmly to the floor and the ceiling, as well as an elaborate two story metal structure draped with long pieces of fabric, spotlights and speakers. She sat sullenly, stirring a weak long island iced tea, and waiting for a barely dressed male to remove even more clothing from his oiled body so that she could slip a five dollar bill into his g-string and fulfill the requirements of the bet she had lost. It was bad enough that she had come right from the courthouse after a trial she was participating in had run long, but it was almost impossible to sit comfortably on a slippery pleather barstool in a pencil skirt. Her skirt rode up every time she shifted even slightly and she would have to try to get a foothold on the stool's lower rungs, in her stiletto heels no less, to lift up slightly to shimmy it back down. She looked like an uptight librarian and she just KNEW that one false move was going to show the room the full-control old lady mega brief underpants that she was wearing to make her over-forty year old ass look good in this damned skirt. At least the suit was red.....red suits always made her feel more powerful in court. The stilettos didn't hurt her confidence, either....just her feet.

Cat tried not to put her arms on the sticky table as she waited, impatiently, for the club host to announce the next performance. At least the place didn't smell like smoke, since the state wide smoking ban had taken effect in Ohio. She begrudgingly admitted that the place smelled nice...like tropical fruit. It was probably one of those top secret aromatherapy blends that made otherwise sane women unable to resist stuffing money in strangers' crotches. Weren't casinos notorious for employing secret scent blends to keep gamblers alert at the tables? It wasn't too far of a stretch to think that Science had found a way to make women drop their cash for beefcake.

She kept slipping her feet on and off of the stool's lower rungs, trying to find a comfortable position to wait out her punishment in the front row of the casino's featured male review show, but she couldn't seem to sit still. She was preoccupied with her case load and the upcoming court appearances she had scheduled for the next few weeks. As a domestic relations attorney, she spent her days helping couples split up their assets and divvy up time with their children, hopefully, without killing each other. Many of the cases involved domestic violence, which required her to be familiar with criminal law, as well, so that she could do her best to protect her clients. It was a lot to keep track of, but Cat was dedicated to doing the best that she could for each and every family that imploded in her office. She had very little time for what she considered to be frivolous entertainment. Strip clubs DEFINITELY ranked right up there on her lift of frivolous things to avoid at all costs.

"Stop fidgeting! The boys are going to think that you don't want to be here," warned Cat's friend Della, with a smirk. Della was sitting on the stool next to Cat, sipping a Pineapple Upside Down Cake martini and grinning like a Cheshire Cat.

"I'm not fidgeting! I am trying to keep MY ass out of the strip show!" Cat said, petulantly. "I am NEVER participating in one of your little betting pools every again. I hate it when you win! You are such an ungracious bitch! You could have at least let me stop at home to change!"

Della threw her head back and laughed uproariously. She laughed so loudly that even the drunk wedding party whooping it up at the next table turned to see what was so funny.

"You shouldn't let your mouth write checks that your ass can't cash! You were the one that said that horse was a sure thing. You said that if he didn't win, you would do anything I wanted for my birthday. Well, Sister, I want to see you stuff that fiver in a sweaty man's banana hammock. You haven't seen a man naked since that snake Giles left to find himself." Della said the last two words in her worst fake British accent using little bunny ears as air quotes. Della hated her ex-husband Giles George Marston the Fourth almost as much as Cat did....almost.

"I couldn't be happier with my life right now!" Cat declared vehemently. "I have two fabulous boys that are almost men, my career has never been more successful and I lost 187 pounds of dumbass when my lame ex-husband left for Europe earlier this year. My life is perfect!"

"Perfectly celibate. What a waste!" Della said with disdain. "You look smoking hot in that fire engine red suit. You would look even hotter if you would lose the camisole and let the girls out to play. That rack of yours could earn you a few tips in this joint. You need to get back on the horse!" Della lifted her drink in a silent salute and finished off the last drops of the sweet cocktail as she slid off of the stool and straightened her tight black skirt. "I am going to the ladies' room, but I fully expect you to save that cash until I get back. If I don't get a picture of this, the Girls will NEVER believe it!"

Cat watched her lifelong friend wind her way through the bar tables full of rowdy women and sighed in resignation. Della was right. She had lost the bet fair and square. She should have just stuck to the bracket. Making the side bet with Della was stupid, but too many Mint Juleps will do that to a girl. That was the last time that she bet on the Kentucky Derby based on the color of the jockey's silks. Pink was her favorite color, but the horse had been a long shot. Time to pay up. At least it was a Thursday night and the place was only full at the front where she and Della were seated. The show would probably be much shorter than it would be on the weekend, since there were only so many women that the dancers could coerce out of their funds.

There was no way that she was riding any of the "horses" in this joint. It was a Male Review, not a cocktail party. It was almost impossible for Cat to enjoy a bunch of mostly naked men gyrating around for her enjoyment when she had two sons not much younger than the dancers on stage. It just felt creepy. Her son Daniel was a sophomore in college and her son Riley was a senior in high school. The fact that women her age where groping the family jewels of boys young enough to be her son made her slightly ill. The sweet cocktail that she was sipping wasn't helping relieve Cat's feelings of discomfort, either. God, she hoped that the show started soon so she could stuff her money into the first g-string that got close enough and get the hell out of there. She had a whole stack of briefs to go through to get ready for court appearances this week....and NONE of them were Fruit of the Loom.

Della returned just as the lights on stage dimmed and the sound of sirens started blaring so loudly that Cat startled and almost slid off of the leather covered stool that she had been trying so hard to remain seated upon. Blue lights started flashing on light bar above the stage and the emcee started yelling through a megaphone.

"Ladies, we have an emergency! There has been a serious crime committed here tonight!" The emcee was hidden somewhere backstage, but the speakers were set up so that his voice was blasted from one end of the half-empty night club to the other. "A known thief has been spotted in the audience. She is a Cat Burglar......and Officer Goodbody is on his way to make the arrest! Everyone, put your hands up.....and then put them together for our first dancer!" screamed the hidden voice.

"Ladies, the Officer is her to make an arrest! Be careful, Ladies! His GUNS are loaded and his NIGHT STICK is a deadly weapon....." screamed the disassociated voice over the sound system. When a spotlight landed on the table, Cat was momentarily blinded. What the hell? A pair of hand landed on her shoulders and spun her around on her stool. She sat with her mouth gaping open as a dark haired man in a Police costume grinned at her and began to move his hips in a circular motion as Della whistled and clapped. When the gentleman grabbed Cat's hand and tried to pull her up, she pulled her hand away and frantically tried to scoot back on her stool. She moved back as far as she could, but the dancer put his hands on her knees and pulled her legs apart, trying to dance close enough to make his gyrating hips look like he was doing lewd things to her lap.

"Oh my GOD! Get off of me!" Cat yelled at the dancer, trying to be heard above the blaring sirens and the wildly screaming women at the surrounding tables. Cat scrambled to pull her skirt down and remove the dancer's hands from her legs, but the stool began to tilt with all of her agitated movements. She felt herself listing to the side, losing her balance as she flailed on the wobbly bar stool. Oh, no! She was going down! Cat lost her balance and felt herself going backwards. She felt a sharp pain at the side of her skull and her last coherent thought was that she was probably going to be arrested for indecent exposure when everyone caught a glimpse of her enormous old lady underwear...

Jackson Capone III loved his life. At the ripe old age of 43, he had attained almost every goal that he had set for himself in this life. He had a brand new luxury condo in a state of the art skyscraper right on the Ohio river. He drove a brand new Nissan 370Z Coupe with the Sports Package. He was rocking the brand new dream job created just for him. He was the Executive Vice President and General Manager of a brand new racino, a combined race track and casino, in Cincinnati, Ohio. The gaming industry was on the cusp of breaking out of the geographically locked traditional cities of Las Vegas, Reno and Atlantic City and Jax was fully prepared to take advantage of the newly formed, untapped Midwest Gaming Market to make a name for himself within his family's gaming empire. Jax had been living in the shadow of his legendary father, Black Jack Cappone, and this new venture was the opportunity that Jax had been waiting for to prove that he was every bit as capable of running a gaming empire as his old man.

Jax deserved this opportunity. He had starting working in his dad's sports book as a runner when he was twelve years old. He had shadowed the old man at work for years before he headed off to college at Cornell for a formal education. He had earned a Bachelor's Degree in Gaming Management at the renown Ivy League university before heading home to Las Vegas to get his dual Masters of Science in Hotel Administration and Masters of Business Administration. Jax knew the casino business through both practical experience and formal education. He was a sure bet as the next leader of his family's gaming empire. Being the only child and heir didn't mean a thing to his father if he couldn't do the work. Too many people depended on CGI for their livelihood and Black Jack was nothing if not loyal to the people that were loyal to him.

Jax was loyal. He knew that it was a matter of "when" not "if" he got the job after his father retired. At 78 years of age, Black Jack Cappone was still vibrant and larger than life, but his wife Vera was making a fuss about wanting to retire. The only job as hard as being the head of a multibillion dollar gaming enterprise was being the spouse of a gaming mogul. Jax's mom Vera had hung in there with his dad for forty four years, but she was ready to relax and enjoy some of the fruits of all of their labor. She had been bugging Black Jack to retire for the last three years, and Jax knew she was making headway. The only logical candidate to step in when Black Jack retired was his only son, Jackson Cappone III. This very example of loving but persistent nagging was exactly why Jax loved his mother. It was also the very reason that he avoided romantic entanglements of any kind.

Women had power over the men in their lives when there was love between them. Jax thought of love as just another commodity that motivated people to make choices in their lives. Jax could rattle off hundreds of examples of men and women meeting their ruin because of what they thought was "love." Love was power. In some cases, love had more destructive power than money, drugs or alcohol. Addictions were easier to shake than "love." Shifting that kind of power to a lover was just too much of a risk for Jax to take. Jax had grown up in a world that revolved around gambling. Watching countless fortunes won and lost had made Jax a very conservative decision maker. Love seemed like a bad bet to Jax.

Just because he had sworn off love did not mean that he didn't enjoy the company of women. Jax had never lacked for female attention. Some of the most beautiful women in the world worked in Las Vegas where he had grown up. While his father and mother had certainly been in a loving relationship, his father had always encouraged Jax to enjoy his time as a single man and all of the benefits that being a casino boss' son entailed.

Women had always flocked to Jax. He knew that his background made him a target for social climbers, but his good looks made heads turn before people even knew his name. Jax never tried to skate by on either his family name or his handsome face. He might have gotten his dark good looks from his mom, but he had gotten his height, his instinct about people and good business sense from his dad. Jax knew that his dad made decisions that affected hundreds, if not thousands, of people every day, but he never made those decisions lightly. He tried his best to be successful and share that success with all of his employees and investors, no matter how small. Jax tried to do the same.

Black Jack had taught his son to treat everyone that he dealt with in a respectful way, whether it was the valet that parked his car or the multi-platinum recording artist that was performing in an exclusive casino show. The same rules applied to the women that shared his time and his bed. Jax may not want a serious permanent relationship, but he always took great pains to be honest with the women he dated and to try to leave them with a smile as the inevitable end of their time together drew near. Jewelry was usually an easy way to bring a smile to a woman's face, in Jax's experience.

When he took over the old man's job as CEO, Jax would have everything that he always wanted. The Cincinnati Project had been three years in the making and Jax had been at the head of the project since the beginning. Working with political lobbyist to ensure that new gaming laws were passed in Ohio had been just the beginning. Before legislation was even passed permitting gambling in the Buckeye State, Jax had been scouting out the perfect location for the property, negotiating with local businesses for services and spending hours working with his architects and contractors to design the perfect vision of a modern race track casino resort. This was no small undertaking with the grand tradition of horse racing in the Ohio River Valley and Cincinnati's proximity to the racing dynasties in Kentucky just a stone's throw across the river. They had to go big or go home.

He was intimately knowledgeable about each and every aspect of the Queen's Run's operations. It was his baby. Jax had tested all of the linens, bathed with all of the hotel's bath products, and approved the décor in all of the different hotel room pricing levels. He had tasted most of the bar's signature drinks and had almost all of the spa treatments demonstrated on him, although he absolutely drew the line at waxing. Just the thought of hot wax near his man junk made him shudder. Manscaping was for braver men than him.

After two years of construction and hundreds of hours on site, the Queen's Run had finally opened its doors. So far, the three months that the Queen's Run Race Track and Casino had been welcoming visitors to the beautiful riverfront location had been wildly successful, outpacing their estimated profit margins by more than seven percent. While it didn't sound like a large increase, when you applied that percentage to the millions of extra dollars that it represented, the Board of Directors of the Cappone Entertainment International was very pleased.

Jax made his was from his plush office on the fourth floor of the casino complex down to the gaming floor to check on the guests. During his nightly walk-through, he couldn't help but smile at the magnificence that was the Queen's Run Race Track and Casino Resort. Everywhere he looked, he saw luxury. The construction of the complex was inspired by the Schonbrunn Palace in Austria, the summer palace of the Hapsburg rulers, which is one of the most beautiful palaces in Europe. The resort prided itself on offering something for everyone that visited.

There was live horse racing, during the Spring and Summer, as well as a Race Book betting area showing simulcast races from across the world that guests could bet on when horses were nor running on the one mile dirt track at the center of the complex. There was a state of the art casino offering any time of gaming table imaginable, plus electronic games for those that didn't want to compete with anyone but a microchip. There was a state of the art spa with a beautiful indoor Olympic sized pool that connected the therapy area with the luxury hotel, concert stage and conference center. There were gourmet restaurants, mid level dining establishments, sports bars and the requisite casino buffet to keep guests energized. There were, in grand Vegas tradition, NO CLOCKS to be found anywhere but the guest rooms. All of it.....every last square inch....was Jax's to make or break. He was determined to succeed.

The newly established Ohio Casino Control Commission was closely scrutinizing all of the budding gambling facilities in the Buckeye State and Jax had to keep a close eye on all areas of the resort's operations. The Queen's Run couldn't afford to have fines levied against them to up the already high opening year operating costs of the luxury gaming facility. He had managed to avoid any contact with organized crime in this part of the country, but he knew that they would still attempt to invade the facility with card counters and prostitutes. It was almost impossible to keep them out, but Jax had recruited veteran management staff from CGI's resorts in Las Vegas, Reno and Atlantic City that could spot a card counter at fifteen paces and knew a working girl from a female guest so he could keep illegal activities out of the Queen's Run. The biggest problem with their brand new facility was making sure that "exiles" were not using their casino to violate their national gaming ban.

The average visitor to a gaming establishment had no idea that there was a nationally monitored database full of the names and pictures of gaming addicts and card counters that were supposed to be banned from all casinos in the United States. This list of exiles was made up of gambling addicts that had entered a treatment program and volunteered to keep themselves out of the places that fed their addictions as well as casino cheats that had been caught trying to beat the House and were no longer welcome by any reputable establishment. Jax had already had the dubious privilege of escorting several banned gamblers, including a Cincinnati City Administrator and School Superintendant that had placed wagers with taxpayer money, from the premises. He hoped that the Queen's Run's tough reputation spread and the hopefuls stopped trying to beat their bans at his resort soon.

The facility had once been a series abandoned Ohio riverfront warehouses that had been taken over by the worst and poorest of Cincinnati's residents. The city's displaced homeless fought with rats, drug runners and prostitutes for shelter in the run down storage facilities that had once been filled with goods for sale in the heyday of the nineteenth century when the Queen City had prospered from rapid river trade along the Ohio river, down to the Mississippi.

No matter what time of day Jax moved through his facility, he caught the eyes of admiring women. Ladies seated at the slot machines turned away from the spinning wheels to watch him walk by in his custom cut black worsted wool suits. Females at the gaming tables stopped contemplating their cards to look him over and smiled at what they saw. At 6'4", Jax stood head and shoulders above most of the ladies and even the gentlemen in the casino and his devastating good looks certainly kept most of the feminine, and some of the masculine, eyes on him as he sauntered confidently thorough his kingdom. He didn't bother to stop, but he was constantly greeting guests as his sweeping gaze checked both the levels of their complimentary cocktails and the piles of chips in front of them, ensuring that they were having a good time or to wish them good luck at the tables. He never lingered, even with guest that he recognized as frequent gamers. He fended off phone numbers being slipped into his pockets and gently, but firmly, shook off several beautifully manicured hands that tried to stall him long enough to secure a later liaison. The women were beautiful. They were also doomed to failure. It wasn't that Jax didn't enjoy the company of women on occasion. He loved women. He also knew that relationships took time. The only lady that Jax had time for these days was the Queen's Run. He was so close to meeting his own goals that he wouldn't allow himself to be distracted by a woman.

As he stopped at the bar to ask the bartenders how the new wait staff was working out, he was momentarily stunned by the sheer size of the liquor display behind the counter. Six floors of top shelf liquor from all over the world that could only be accessed by the bartender through a specially designed lift system never ceased to amaze and amuse visitors to the gaming floor main bar, including Jax himself. Jax loved to try to stump the bartenders by asking how to mix obscure drinks, but he had yet to find a cocktail that the veteran staff didn't know how to mix with flair. He was going to have to start doing random internet searches to find classic cocktails if he ever wanted to get the bartenders to consult the state of the art mixology software that he had personally approved the funds for. So far, if was gathering cyber dust because he had done such a good job with hiring veteran drink slingers.

Just as he was thinking of ordering an obscure mixed drink from the 1920's known as a Hock Cobbler, just to be obnoxious, the phone in the breast pocket of his custom tailored suit coat vibrated. He slipped the phone from the silk lined inside breast pocket and read the display identifying Tom Hanley, the manager of Jester's Night Club. Jax swiped his finger across the phone's touch display and greeted his colleague.

"Hi, Tom. What's up?" Jax kept walking toward the elevators that would take him down to the plush gaming area as he waited to hear what had prompted his normally competent night club manager to seek him out during prime club business hours.

"Hey, Boss man. We have a problem." Jax could tell by the serious tone of Tom's voice that something bad had happed. His heart beat sped up as he waited for Tom to get to the point. "A guest fell off of her chair during one of the performances and knocked herself out on one of bar tables, but she is refusing medical treatment. She was unconscious briefly, so I called for the ambulance, per protocol, but she won't let them examine her. Mike and Bobby from security carried her into the second floor first aid suite, but she is awake now and demanding that we let her leave."

Jax arrived at the elevator and punched the button several times in agitation as he responded, "I'll be right there. Don't let her leave." He put his phone back into his breast pocket and hit the elevator's down button a few more times, like it would speed the car's arrival. When the elevator's indicator lit up with the down arrow and the door slid open, Jax quickly jumped in and pushed the button for the second floor. In the fifteen seconds that it took for the elevator car to travel down two floors, Jax had already run several worst case scenarios through his head for what this accident could mean for his budding casino. He needed to call legal, make sure that an accident report was completed by any staff that were witnesses, get statements from any guests that has caught a glimpse of the events that led up to the accident, anything and everything that he could gather to prevent the injured guest from milking a minor accident for a major cash payout. Hell, this could even be one of those "slip and fall" cons where someone expected a big cash payout for "soft tissue" injuries that they claimed after they left the scene without a thorough medical exam.

Jax was mentally gearing up to placate the con artist refusing to have her head examined in the security office when he reached the appropriate door heard a woman's raised voice competing with the lower, soothing tones of several more masculine voices. Jax rapped his knuckles three times on the door before using his key card to open the lock and stride confidently into the fray. The site that greeted him made every thought in his head go completely blank.

A beautiful woman was holding a pen like a sword and swinging it at everyone that came within a foot of where she was sitting behind the small fiberboard desk. Her hair was a glossy sable and her eyes were bright blue. He could see the contrast even from across the room. She was magnificent....but she was pissed! Stunned, Jax just stood, with one foot inside the doorway and his hand seemingly glued to the door handle.

"You cannot keep me here! You are not police officers and I am not under suspicion of having committed a crime! I want to leave RIGHT NOW!" The brunette was breathing really hard, making her more than generous breasts strain the buttons on her fire engine red suit coat. She had one hand holding the side of her head and the other swinging a fountain pen like a rapier at everyone in the room to make her point.

All eyes turned toward him as the door opened. Jax cleared his throat and tried to remember why he had been summoned to the scene in the first place. It was a rare event when Jax lost his almost legendary composure and he pulled on all of his sophisticated business executive reserves to get his big head back into the game that his little head had attempted to highjack. He managed to find his voice and declare, "Ma'am, my name is Jackson Cappone and I am the Property Manager. I understand that there has been an accident?"

The angry flash of blue eyes focused on him in such a rage that a lesser man would have grabbed his nuts to make sure that they hadn't shrunk into tiny little raisins, like she was clearly willing them to do. Oh, his little head was hiding its head in fear now. "I am FINE, as I keep telling your Rent-a-cops, and I want to leave NOW!" she demanded. "And where is Della? What have you done with my friend?"

Jax raised his hands up, palms out, in a show of placation as he moved further into the tense office scene. He looked briefly at the two enormous bouncers that served as security for the night club. They were both leaning against the wall as far from the furious female as they could be without abandoning their posts, but both men had the terrified look of rookies about to flee from a combat situation.

Jax reached down into his memory banks for the training he had received in management school about diffusing conflict situations. If he remembered correctly, everyone was supposed to move as slowly as possible and remove any unnecessary bystanders from the scene. He briefly made eye contact with the two cowering security specialists and flicked his head toward the exit.

"Thanks for the assistance, but I think Tom and I can take it from here, gentlemen" Jax said in his most soothing tone. He flicked his gaze between the woman wielding the not-so-deadly weapon and Mike and Dave. When neither security professional made any indication that they had heard him at all, he raised his voice and tried, again, to get their attention.

"Guys?!" he snapped, still waiting for the two big lugs leaning against the office wall to acknowledge him, waving his arm indicating that they should get out. He figured that clearing the room of potential victims from Princess Poison Pen was probably a good idea right now. They finally caught his extremely unsubtle cues and headed out of the door like their asses were on fire, avoiding any eye contact.

"Tom, can you give me the status?" Jax asked as he turned his gaze to the Club Manager that was cowering in the corner of the office looking like he might just cry. Angry feminine growling came from the desk area and the pen that had finally been pointing down at the desk was suddenly pointed right at him.

"I will tell you the status! I want to leave here immediately and this skunk in a cheap suit," she yelled, swinging her pen scepter toward Tom, flinching behind a faux fichus in the corner, "is telling me that I cannot leave until I am checked out by a doctor AND have been released by the Casino Manager. You cannot keep me here! I am not signing ANYTHING and I don't have to! Even with a blow to the head I know that this is TOTAL BULLSHIT! I will press charges if you do not let me out of this fucking place RIGHT NOW!" With the last two loudly voiced words, the woman jumped out of the low office chair and started to march around the desk toward the door Jax was standing in front of.

Princess Poison Pen's big eruption seemed to take all of the energy that she had and her face started to turn white as she stumbled slightly and reached to grab the edge of the desk that she had just walked around. As she came closer, Jax realized that she wasn't anywhere near as tall as her personality made her appear. In fact, even with the sky high sexy red pumps she was wearing, the little firebrand wouldn't even hit his chin. Her angry stride slowed to a halt she began to sway on her feet. The woman's face grimaced in pain and she clutched her head with the hand that wasn't swinging her ink-filled weapon of choice. As she began to buckle at the knees, an alarmed Jax took two giant steps across the beige industrial carpet to grab her around the waist before she hit the floor.

The woman that had just been spitting fire was slumped, moaning, against his chest. Her head lay right over his heart and he could feel the traitorous organ begin to speed up with the adrenalin that saving this woman from falling had sent through his system. It was just the tension and excitement of the moment, he told himself. It had absolutely nothing to do with the fact that the woman that he was holding in his arms was the most fascinating woman he had laid eyes on in as long as he could remember. Jax leaned down to lift her into his arms so that he could get her somewhere comfortable. He tried to ignore the fact that she was so soft and her hair smelled like exotic wild flowers. She was injured, damn it! This was not the time to be sniffing her intoxicating scent.

Sign up for Cate's newsletter at

www.catebeaumont.com/newsletter for more information on the upcoming release, in person appearances, contests, sneak peeks, and more!

If you enjoyed this book, please consider leaving a review so that other readers can find and enjoy Cate's books!

ABOUT THE AUTHOR

Cate Beaumont is a mild-mannered tax attorney by day and a steamy contemporary romance writer at night.

After planning educational seminars and writing boring Legal tomes for several years, she decided to turn her love of romance novels and book conventions into a job! She is the author of Lucky Strike, Book 1 in the Lucky, Kentucky series which is making its way around the romance world via all of the major ebook retailers. Cate is also known to wear incredibly ostentatious tiaras whenever she thinks she can get away with it.

Cate Loves To Hear From Readers You Can Get In Touch Here:

www.catebeaumont.com
cate@catebeaumont.com